Earth

K.C. MCMILLIAN

Kiana (K.C.) McMillian

Dedication

I dedicate this to you. And if no one has told you today, you're amazing.

Table of Contents

Chapter 1

Confessions of a Teenage Witch

Dear Diary,

I am writing in this diary because Ms. Hudson advised that I use this as a coping mechanism to eliminate my aggression. I am debating whether transferring my thoughts onto paper will work, but I'll try. What do I have to lose?

It has been eight weeks since someone murdered my father, and the police still have not caught the person who did it.

Just like they swept Destiny's mother's and Isabel's parents' deaths under the rug, the police seem to have given up on solving my father's murder. I haven't attended school in over a week and don't eat or sleep. I keep thinking about who could have murdered my father and why. On the dreadful day my father died, he had something clenched in his fist. I retrieved it from his hand when the paramedics weren't looking and hid it in my pocket. It was a flash drive. I haven't looked at it yet because I am not ready to see what is on it, but I have it in a safe place. I don't care about anything other than finding out who murdered my father. But here's a turn of events. Gabriella calls me daily, and Kevin and I aren't on good terms.

The Witch Council summoned me for a meeting tomorrow because I told my friends about magic. What they don't know is that my magic has grown over the weeks, so if they think I'll let them remove it, they can think again.

"Good morning, Claudette," Kevin greets me as I walk to the sofa. "Do you plan on eating breakfast today—or ever?"

I don't look at him as I pick up the remote and flip through the channels. A few days after the funeral and my first phone call from Eli's irritating mother, I overheard Tanya and Tristan discussing the Witch Council's plan to remove my magic with Kevin, and he agreed with them. I know that telling my friends about magic is against the rules, but I hoped my *boyfriend* would support me no matter what. But apparently, he doesn't think I can control my emotions and believes I shouldn't possess such powers as a new witch. Since overhearing that conversation, our relationship has been on the rocks. The council, including Ms. Hudson, didn't approve of my two best friends accompanying me to the funeral, and now they want to take my magic away using a spell and a ceremonial knife known as a *Ce-Ja*. All because I took Kevin's car, drove to my old hometown to pick up my friends, and brought them to Mashalville for the funeral. I didn't care about the rules then, and I don't care about them now. I trust Nicolette and Spencer with my life—about the only two people I do trust—and I know they would never betray me.

"How long are you going to give me the silent treatment?" Kevin presses.

I snort. "Why should I talk to you?"

"What is your issue, Claudette?" He walks towards me cautiously.

"My issue? What. Is. My. Issue?" I spit out slowly through gritted teeth.

His lips twist into a frown, and I can tell he chooses his words carefully when he speaks. "Claudette, I know you miss your father. But this is not the way to act. I haven't done anything to you, and I can't help but think you're blaming me for something."

I throw my head back and descend into uncontrollable laughter. *Is he serious? He really doesn't know?*

"Really, Kevin? Are we going to pretend you don't know why I am upset? I know you were angry about my friends being here. Am I supposed to act as if I am okay with you siding with the Witch Council?" I hiss.

"Claudette, humans aren't supposed to know about magic! If that's why you're upset, I suggest you get over it! Because I am not changing my stance on it."

"Noted!" I jump to my feet, rushing out of the room. I get my already-packed bag from the closet and use my magic to take me to Eli's house. That argument was all I needed to solidify my decision to leave.

I understand the rules are there for a reason, and I get that just because I trust Nicolette and Spencer doesn't mean everyone else will or can. But how could they think I wouldn't want my two best friends from childhood to be by my side as I said goodbye to my father? I didn't tell them that the town was full of magic; I told them I had magic and that my mother had it. I also told them someone murdered my father, and no one in this god-forsaken town knows who! Yes, I revealed some secrets, but not all, and the fact that my *"boyfriend"* can't be on my side is a deal breaker for me.

(A text message between Kevin and Tanya)

Kevin:

> **Hey, you need to locate Claudette. NOW!**

She just left, and I have no idea where she went.

Tanya:

Are you serious? You were to watch her.

What are we supposed to do now?

The Witch Council wants to see her tomorrow.

Kevin:

What do you expect me to do with no magic?

She's powerful.

You need to conduct the ceremony ASAP.

Tanya:

You best pull out your charm and reel her back in.

Kevin:

It's too late!

She knows I've sided with the Witch Council to take her magic away.

And I am tired of keeping up this façade.

Tanya:

Stick to the plan, Kevin!

We almost have what we want.

Chapter 2
Earth Witches

Appearing in the middle of Eli's living room with no official warning, he jumps to his feet from the sofa, startled by my sudden intrusion.

He holds a blanket in front of his lower half to cover himself. "Claudette, what are you doing here?" he asks, snapping his fingers as sweatpants appear on his legs.

My cheeks grow hot, and I shake away the sudden dirty thoughts that threaten to invade my mind. "Where are we with pinpointing who killed my father?"

He glances at my bag. "Why are you here with a duffle bag? And we don't answer a question with another question, Claudette." His lips curve into one of his dashing smiles, but his eyes remain serious.

"Oh. I was just in the neighborhood and thought I'd stop by to see how the investigation was going." He sees right through my lousy excuse. "Um... can I stay here?" I ask softly.

"Why do you want to stay here?" He presses. "Did something happen between you and Kevin?"

Lowering my eyes to the floor, my heart descends to the pit of my stomach.

Kevin had been caring until he wasn't. He became distant and cold after I invited my friends to be my support system for my dad's funeral. From that moment on, our relationship deteriorated. Even the sex felt strained and forced—something to keep me craving him—but he did not want me. I guess telling my friends about my magic was a "deal breaker" for him. Still, my gut tells me that he got what he desired from me, and now he's done, especially now that I'm damaged goods. However, if it was that easy for him to withdraw from me, perhaps he never truly loved me in the first place. Maybe he was only telling me what I wanted to hear to get what was precious to me!

The day after my father's funeral, I had dinner with Nicolette, Spencer, and Eli. We discussed the truth spell and deliberated Kevin's reactions. Nicolette still believed he was the perfect guy for me until she spoke to him at the funeral, and he gave her the cold shoulder. He was nothing like the caring and loving person who took me to my hometown for ice cream with my friends. Spencer was skeptical, and I was sure he thought I had lost my mind until I showed him my magic. They asked Eli if he had powers, too, but he shrugged them off and said that only I had them. I did not blame him for lying. Just because I disclosed my magic to them does not mean he had to. Eli wasn't pleased with me for telling my friends about magic. Still, he did not turn on me like Kevin did. Eli still shows his unwavering support, and according to him, the prophecy foretold that he and I were meant to be together, not Kevin and me.

"Claudette?" Eli calls out my name, taking me away from my inner thoughts.

He walks toward me, arms open, and I fall into his embrace, letting his strong arms wrap around me while I sob. It's easy to be vulnerable with Eli. He hasn't judged me unless it was about Kevin, and even then, he did it out of concern for my well-being. I inhale his familiar scent, feeling safe and protected in his arms, until waves of electricity flow from his body to mine, our magic uniting.

"Will you stop doing that?" I say, pushing him away.

His lips curl into a sexy smile. "I'm not doing it on purpose. Our magic is connecting."

Heat rises to my face, and I look away immediately with guilt.

Eli regards me through narrowed eyes. "Are you going to tell me what happened between you and Kevin?" he asks, his tone gentle but firm.

My eyes fill with water again, and tears stream down my cheeks before I can stop them. "Kevin and I broke up. I have nowhere else to go."

Eli's stern expression softens, and he doesn't press further. "You can stay with me for as long as you need. We can be roommates."

"Thank you." I wipe away my tears and manage a small smile before masking my feelings. "How close are we to finding out who killed my father?"

Eli has grown used to my shift in emotions, so he thinks nothing of it and disappears to his room to retrieve a notebook and pen.

He flips through the pages. "Honestly, Claudette, I don't know where to start. We don't have any solid leads."

Observing his notes closer, I notice he still has Kevin's name circled as the murderer.

Screwing up my face, I place my hands on my hips. "Why is Kevin still a suspect if we have no leads, Eli?"

Eli sucks in the air and exhales slowly, choosing his words carefully. "Because, Claudette, he hesitated when you asked him if he knew who killed your father. The potion had timed out, so that means he knows more than he's letting on. His hesitation wouldn't have happened if he were still under the spell."

"You don't think he killed my father? But he knows who did?"

"It's a possibility we can't ignore."

The mystery of my father's death is becoming more complex by the minute. I don't want to believe that my boy—*ex-boyfriend* could be involved.

Was Eli right all along about Kevin?

The people crossed off my list of suspects are the ones whose alibis were accounted for during my father's murder. The twins and Gabriella were at the movies; they knew my father, and I had a date planned. Lin was taking piano lessons. Ms. Hudson was late to our therapy session because she was with Mr. Handsome. Kevin didn't feel well and was fighting with Eli. And Destiny and Isabel were on a date.

I have half a mind to create more truth potion, administer it to everyone, and directly ask if they killed my father, but Eli advised against it. He warned that although the potion forces the truth out of people, there is a spell that can be cast to counteract its effects. *Go figure! Magic has its limits.* What else can I do? It has been weeks, and I am not any closer to finding the murderer, or rather, the detectives aren't any closer. They are likely to write it off as a cold case soon, like Isabel's parents and Destiny's mom. I don't know much about the law or how it works in a town of witches cloaked in the real world. *Nothing here seems realistic!*

Eli meets my gaze with a solemn expression, pondering before finally speaking. "My mother was alerted when you made the 911 call."

My brows snap together. "What?"

"She listens in on all the 911 calls made in town," he admits.

Folding my arms across my chest, I ask, "Is that even legal?"

Eli shrugs. "It's supposed to be against the law, but are you going to tell her that? In a town like this, who knows what's legal and what's not?"

This town doesn't follow the basic rules of life!

"When I heard the call, I left to confront Kevin about it," Eli continues.

Rolling my eyes. "We know how that turned out," I mutter under my breath.

My phone vibrates in my pocket, interrupting our conversation.

Tanya is calling me. *What does she want?*

"Are you going to answer that?" Eli raises an eyebrow.

Shaking my head, I ignore the call. "We need to figure out who killed my fa—"

My phone vibrates again, and this time, I answer it while Eli draws a new circle with my dad's name in the center. He adds arrows to a question mark as a suspect.

Tanya demands I attend tomorrow's council meeting, or they will drag me there kicking and screaming! I hang up on her so fast that I almost break the screen.

Who does she think she is, ordering me around like that?

Eli's brows shoot up, overhearing Tanya. "I guess there's a meeting tomorrow that demands our attendance."

Shaking my head. "No. You should go to school. I'll handle it."

"*Both* of us should be in school," he reasons, grabbing my shoulders. "I'm going with you, Claudette. I'm not going to let you face this alone, and I'll be there as a friend and nothing more."

"Thank you." I sigh under his steady gaze.

Eli is a really great guy, and I wish I met him first.

"Unless..." He smirks suggestively.

"Unless *what*?" I raise an eyebrow.

"Unless you want something more between us."

"Are you flirting with me during a time of crisis, Elijah Powers?" I crack a smile.

"Of course not, Claudette Richardson," he chuckles. "Just making sure you know all your options."

Rolling my eyes playfully, I nudge him. "Let's focus on the task at hand before we start discussing anything else," I say, trying to keep our priorities straight. "You should probably add Kevin's parents as suspects as well."

As great as Eli is, I am not ready to dive into anything more than a friendship with him just yet. And I don't want him to be a rebound. He is too special of a guy for that.

"Will do," he responds with a nod, scribbling down their names and catching my gaze with a reassuring smile. He understands and respects my feelings, which only makes me appreciate him more.

He motions for me to follow him down the hallway.

With my bag in hand, I swiftly trail behind, eager to discover my new bedroom. Eli and his brother Jeremiah shared the two-bedroom, two-bath apartment until Jeremiah got his own place and moved out. This is convenient for me because I need a place to stay. Gabriella made it clear I couldn't live with them, although I'm sure my father left the house for me. However, I am still a minor, but even if the law were enforced in Mashalville, I wouldn't want to live there anyway. I hate all of them! *Hate* is a strong word, but you've been following along, haven't you?

Gabriella agrees that the twins and I shouldn't live under the same roof. *There is no argument there.* Also, that's the last place my father was alive.

Eli opens the door for me, and I exhale slowly, studying the space before me. The room is painted royal blue with a bunch of Marvel characters plastered on the walls and a significant crescent moon engraved with the letters JP. A twin-size bed with no sheets and covers sits in the center, although a full-size bed could be a better fit for the room.

"I'll leave you to get settled in," he says, giving me a small smile.

I thank him again before he closes the door behind him.

Standing in the room, I close my eyes. The room smells of lavender, giving it a relaxing feel. Snapping my fingers, leopard bedding appears on the bed. Did I mention I love being a witch? Because I do! I envision a brown wall to complement the bedding, and the walls transform from royal blue to a warm chocolate brown. Thinking about a small desk, it appears in the corner of the room. I put my bag on the bed to unpack my Dell laptop and place it on the newly manifested desk. Unfortunately, magic has its limits, so I have to manually remove the posters from the walls.

Two hours later, the room is starting to feel like mine, and I'm settling in nicely.

Sitting on my new bed, I decide to finally look through the flash drive my dad left me; my answers may very well be on there. Between dwelling on who murdered my father and silently battling with Kevin, I have put this off long enough. It is time.

Unzipping the side pocket of my blue and black duffel bag, I grab my jewelry box and place it on the desk. Holding my breath for a moment, I sigh before opening and pulling out the flash drive. I contemplate whether I should plug it into my laptop or not. *Do it!* My inner voice, Detta, urges me, so I open my computer, turn it on, and insert the flash drive into the USB port. Here goes nothing!

The contents of the device load onto my screen, displaying a series of files. Tapping my fingers nervously on the desk, I wait for the files to fully load. This drive has my father's entire life condensed into folders of information, and it's going to take me hours to go through it all. Maybe even days. There are folders labeled with dates, names, and places. The one that catches my eye is labeled *Chance,* my father's name.

Double-clicking on the folder with his name, I begin reading through the files. His mother was an Earth witch, and his father was a Moon witch. According to this document, the parent with the stronger heart determines the magic their child inherits. My grandmother was an Earth witch, and so was my father. And I was lucky enough, depending on how you look at it, to become an Earth witch as well. After my dad's seventeenth birthday, his parents were murdered, and he fled from this town. *Why are everyone's parents being murdered?* I don't get it!

Earth witches were feared, but the council did not come after him because he chose to be a norm. Back then, Earth witches were viewed as a threat. For decades, they were hunted and murdered by a secret cult of evil witches. *How could they let this go on for all these years?*

Scrolling through all the pictures of the Earth witches that were slain, I fight to hold back tears. Taking a deep breath and exhaling slowly, I continue reading. The witches were murdered with a Ce-Ja dagger.

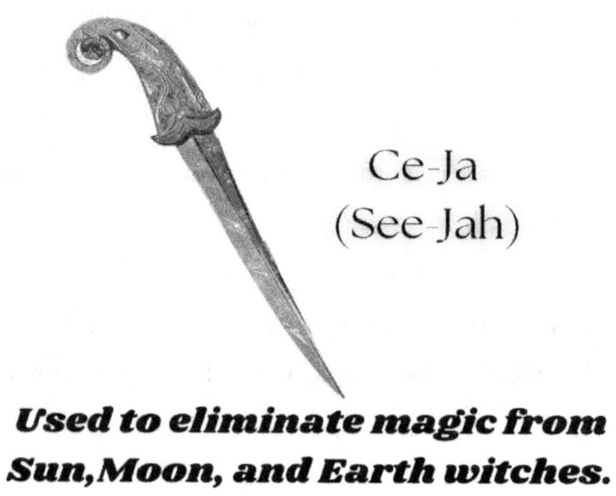

Used to eliminate magic from Sun, Moon, and Earth witches.

There is a subfolder labeled *The Daggers*. Clicking on it, there are pictures and descriptions of a few different daggers with names I cannot pronounce, each with a distinct purpose—all for me to study. A Ne-aik-eart was used to murder Earth witches and absorb their magic. The dagger is gold, black, green, and brown.

Ne-aik-eart
(Knee-Ike-erth)

Used to absorb Earth magic.

Although my father did not practice magic, he was born an Earth witch, which made him a target. The monster who murdered him used the Ne-aik-eart on him and absorbed his magical essence, and it is a matter of time before I am the next victim. Except I'll be ready! The magical autopsy Destiny illegally performed on my father revealed that his wounds were inflicted by this dagger. However, whoever did it masked his stab wounds with magic to cover their tracks. *Jerk!*

Exiting out of the *Chance* folder altogether, I scroll down until I see *Claudia,* my mother's name. My mom was born a Moon witch; so was her father, and her mother was a Sun witch. I recall my dad telling me that her parents died in a car accident, but this file indicates that they were also murdered for a ritual. Ne-aik-oon is the name of the dagger that was used on my grandmother, and it is black and white.

Used to absorb Moon magic.

The gold and yellow dagger used to remove Sun witches' powers is called Ne-aik-un.

Used to absorb Sun magic.

Browsing through unsettling photos of my grandparents and the other brutally murdered witches, my heart breaks. Their hearts were ripped out of their chests, their eyes carved out, and the blood drained from their bodies.

Only the witches who accepted their magic were murdered in this gruesome manner. Since my father wanted to remain a norm, he did not succumb to the same awful fate. *Or did he?*

He is dead. Holding my chest, I choke back the rising panic. Yet Destiny assured me that his body was not completely drained of blood and did not have any open wounds that were visible to the naked eye. I really don't know what happened to my father, and after reading through his files, I'm more confused than before.

My heart shatters for all the witches who suffered at the hands of the secret cult, especially for my grandparents, whom I never got to know. It is beyond me that these *monsters* haven't been brought to justice yet.

I remove the flash drive from my laptop, put it back in my jewelry box, and hide it underneath my mattress. I need time to process all of the information I uncovered.

Pools of tears well up in my eyes, and I want to run to Eli for comfort. Unfortunately, he is in bed, so I opt for a shower instead and hop into bed after letting the warm water wash away some of the pain. With my brain reeling with all the information I have learned, hopefully, I will be able to rest.

Chapter 3

Take my Magic Away, I

Think Not!

The next morning, my stomach is in knots as I prepare for the impending doom with the council. It is foolish for them to think they can take away my magic. Of course, this is the Witch Council I'm going up against. They are seasoned in their magic, and I have only been practicing for a couple of months. However, working with Eli has prepared me for any challenges they may throw my way.

Mrs. Powers withdrew her offer to add me to the council, which is fine because I never wanted to be a part of their stuffy group anyway. Eli's choice to go against his parents scores him major points in my book; he has shown me his loyalty, no matter the repercussions. He disagrees with my decision, but he is still standing by me. Kevin, on the other hand, has not reached out to me since I left. It has only been a day, but his silence speaks volumes. He is my supposed soulmate, according to his version of the prophecy, yet my decision has made him distant from me.

While Eli gets dressed for the council meeting, I wait in the kitchen. Toying with my phone in my hand, I debate whether to text Kevin or not. *Just do it!* Detta urges. I ultimately decide to send him a quick message in an attempt to bridge the gap between us. I am still upset with him, but did my feelings for him disappear overnight? Of course not.

Me:

A few uneasy minutes pass before I double-text him.

Me:

Tapping my foot anxiously, I wait for his response, but it never comes. *Excellent!* Now, I am coming off as desperate. I sigh in frustration, sending one final message. *Fine!* Our relationship is clearly over.

Me:

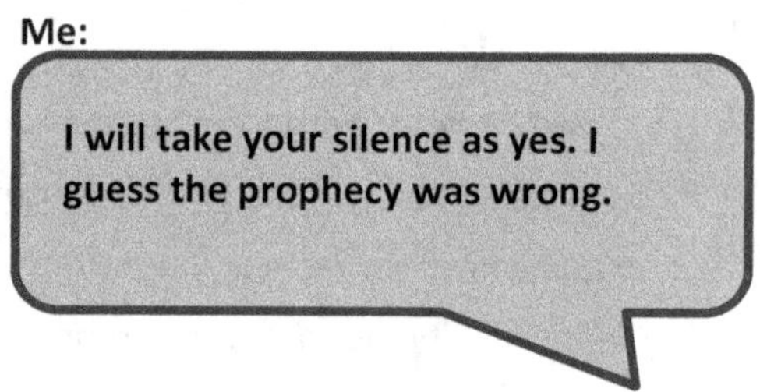

No response. I toss my phone in my bag and shrug my shoulders. It is what it is!

Eli walks into the kitchen, smiling from ear to ear. "Good morning,

Sunshine."

I give him a half-hearted smile. "Why are you in a great mood for 'doomsday?'" I gesture air quotes around the word doomsday.

Folding his arms across his chest, Eli chuckles. "Why are you being so dramatic this early in the morning?"

Rolling my eyes, I tie my locs in a bun. "I'm just not in the mood for sunshine and rainbows today. The Witch Council wants to take my magic!"

His smile fades. "You're not alone in this. Destiny, Lin, and I will help fight the cause with you. There is no way they will take your magic away without casting a vote first."

It is sweet that he is hopeful, but let's be honest, I'm not going to win.

Screwing up my face. "I need a plan, Eli, not blind optimism. Most of the council wants to rid me of my magic. I am not sure how voting will help me when the majority is against me!" I shout, throwing my hands in the air. "Tanya, Tristan, your parents, and your brother are all in favor of team *no magic*. I don't know Ms. Hudson's stance, and the other guy goes with the flow."

"You mean Jimmy?"

"Who cares about his name?!" I shout, "He's just another vote against me!"

Eli puts a comforting hand on my shoulders. "Don't worry, Claudette. It is my birthright to be a part of the Witch Council, and I have formally accepted my role as a member to vote against them. I have also recruited Destiny and Lin. My parents offered them positions on the council months ago, but they declined until now. They have taken their rightful place alongside me to vote in your favor." He gives me a reassuring smile, optimistic that his plan will actually work. "You are the only Earth witch in town that we know of, which naturally deems you a member by default. I know the rules like the back of my hand. Trust me, Claudette. I will not let you down."

His eyes are so sincere that I am in awe. Yet, I am still doubtful. Nonetheless, I entwine my fingers with his. "Let's kick some Witch Council butt!" I am standing my ground against those who seek to suppress my magic.

He squeezes my hand gently, and we head to his car to drive to our impending doom.

Kevin catches my eye, and I can't help but take a sharp breath once we arrive at the town hall. His face is stern, in stark contrast to that usual sexy smile. He's standing in front of the building with his guard dogs, Tanya and Tristan. I guess this is his reason for not texting me back; he was with his trusted minions. Tanya lightly brushes her hand against Kevin's. She whispers something into his ear, changing his facial expression from stern to soft in a matter of seconds. *That is odd.*

A slight pang of jealousy surfaces in my chest. Pushing the feeling aside, I march behind Eli to the entrance of the building, walking past Kevin and avoiding his direction. He grasps my arm before I can fully pass by.

Jerking my arm away, I shoot him a questioning look.

"Can we talk?" he asks.

"No." My answer is firm and final. "I tried talking to you before, but you ignored me. Keep that same energy!"

Tanya's eyes are wide at our exchange. Kevin tries again to grab my arm, but I step back out of his reach. "I have nothing to say to you," I state firmly, turning to walk inside for what I believe will be a showdown.

When I enter the room, a bustling sea of whispers and stares surrounds me. It seems like the entire town of Mashalville is here, waiting for a decision to be made. *Shouldn't they be in school? Or working?*

The ballroom is a grand spectacle where the council members conduct ceremonies and rituals. Tanya and Tristan lower into their seats with the rest of the council. Mrs. Elizabeth Powers takes the stage front and center.

"We are gathered here today to address Miss Richardson's insubordinate actions." She announces from the podium through gritted teeth. Her eyes zero in on Eli. "I see my son is in attendance. For what purpose, I wonder?"

"I am here to advocate for Claudette, mother!" He spits out defiantly.

The room gasps in unison.

Her lips curl into a scowl as she fixes her gaze on Eli. Dismissing his words, she retrieves a large book with a crescent moon engraved on the front cover. The book is black and white, and I watch closely as she flips through the pages. She eyes me warily, reaching into her bag and pulling out a dagger—the Ce-Ja dagger—and sitting it on top of the book.

She builds momentum by pacing back and forth, her eyes never leaving mine. "We—"

"We should cast a vote!" Eli interjects, cutting his mother off.

Mrs. Powers laughs dryly in Eli's direction. "*Now* you are on the Witch Council?"

Eli nods.

"Cast a vote on *what*?" Mrs. Powers sneers with annoyance laced in her tone.

Eli carefully approaches her, taking the dagger away. He gives his mother a stern look, and she reluctantly stands down. *What was that about?*

"Claudette Richardson is innocent," Eli asserts. "Her father was murdered, and she reached out to the two people she trusts the most. As a town, we should sympathize with her, not condemn her. She did not disclose to her friends that this is a town full of witches; she only disclosed her magic to them. And, of course, as it is wrong and against the rules, she needed her two best friends to mourn."

Eli's announcement did not seem to sit well with everyone in the room.

Mr. Powers whispers into his wife's ear, and she exhales before speaking. "Fine. All in favor of eliminating Claudette's magic because she broke our number one rule. Raise your left hand."

Everyone in the crowd raises their left hand, including Kevin.

Jimmy, Ms. Hudson, Eli, Destiny, and Lin are the only ones who keep their hands down. Eli did not expect this. But I did.

It is flattering that Eli wanted to represent me; however, it is time I show this town what I am capable of. Clearing my throat, I shake off the nerves and turn my stern gaze toward the crowd as I take the stage to plead my case.

"Excuse me, the town of Mashalville; I would like to speak for myself regarding the matter."

Mrs. Powers is about to intervene, but I wave my hand, and she plunges to the floor. The crowd gasps. *No more playing nice.*

"The focus of this town is futile! My father was murdered eight weeks ago, and instead of focusing on who killed him, the town wants to remove my magic. How does that make any sense?" I shout, not expecting anyone to answer.

My eyes lock with Ms. Hudson's. "I strongly advise you to leave the room, as this may be a conflict of interest if you wish to remain my therapist," I say, my voice steady.

Ms. Hudson covers her mouth in shock. I have the undivided attention of the room. Even Eli is looking at me with wide eyes. Mrs. Powers is now standing, and she retaliates by using her magic to aim a knife at my heart. I effortlessly catch the knife, an ominous grin spreading on my face. *Too slow.*

There's a switch in my emotions. A weight of guilt lifts off my heavy heart, and I no longer care about the consequences. My brown eyes darken, and my energy shifts into something sinister and more powerful. I feel empowered. All I care about is finding my father's killer and why he was murdered in cold blood.

With a flick of my wrist, I send the knife flying back towards Mrs. Powers, stopping just short of making contact. The room falls silent as Mrs. Powers stares at me with widened eyes.

"I will not hesitate to kill you if you do that again!" I shout, my voice echoing through the room.

"Who do you think you are talking to like that?" Mrs. Powers demands, clenching her fists, but she appears visibly shaken.

Laughing dryly in response to her idiotic question, I snap my fingers, and the knife disappears from sight. And while all eyes are on me, Eli stores the Ce-Ja dagger in his pocket.

Clearing my throat. "Listen up, townspeople of Mashalville! No one will be taking away my magic! And if you try, I *will* kill you. You have been warned."

Ms. Hudson intervenes, her eyes filled with concern. "Claudette, perhaps we should speak in private?"

"No. That won't be necessary." My expression remains neutral, dismissing her request.

Eli confronts me with a worried expression. "Are you okay, Claudette? You just threatened the entire town. They could rebel against you."

"I'm aware. And I've never been better, my friend," I assure him gleefully, nudging his broad shoulder.

"Are you sure?"

Rolling my eyes. "I know what I'm doing, Eli."

"She broke the rules!" Crissy shouts from the crowd, pointing an accusing finger at me. "The council needs to strip her magic away!"

Did I hear Crissy talk? *She never speaks.*

Her outburst takes me by surprise, and my eyes narrow as I focus on her. Perhaps she doesn't realize how serious I am about my warning to this ridiculous town.

"My mother's magic was removed! Claudette's magic should be stripped, too. People outside of this town are not supposed to know about magic! She broke the rules!" Marissa yells, backing up her twin and charging towards me.

Soaring through the herd of people, I meet her head-on.

This is the last time I will allow her and her demon twin to speak to me without consequence.

My mind focuses on her knee, calculating the exact angle and force needed to incapacitate her without causing permanent damage and with just a thought.

Crack.

Marissa collapses to the ground, clutching her knee in agony. "What did you do to me?!" she screams, glaring up at me with pure hatred in her eyes.

I smile, knowing that she will think twice before crossing me again.

Crissy charges at me, her chest heaving with anger as she lunges forward. I sidestep her attack.

Ankles.

Crissy falls to the ground, writhing in pain as she clutches her broken ankles. "You're crazy!" she cries out, tears streaming down her face.

It's a lesson they won't soon forget. With a mere thought, I broke Marissa's knee and both of Crissy's ankles.

"That is my last and final warning!" I declare loudly, my voice cold and unwavering.

Storming out of the room, Destiny, Eli, and Lin scurry behind me. I am livid. This town had the audacity to try to take away my magic. *Mine!* And no one seems to care about the murder of my father, not even the detectives. It is up to me to get to the bottom of it, and once I do, I will kill him or her—*or them!*

"What happened in there, Claudette?" Destiny asks, a crease forming between her eyebrows. "Your anger will eventually consume you into darkness if you don't find a way to channel it."

Choosing not to reply, I walk toward Eli's car and climb into the passenger seat.

"Is she not going to respond to me?" Destiny looks between Eli and Lin, who both shrug.

The rage I am feeling is unfathomable. I never thought about killing anyone—until *now.* I need to get back to Eli's place to unravel more information from the flash drive. The file has so many folders, and I must go through them all.

Eli says bye to Lin and Destiny and gets into the driver's seat. He doesn't start the car right away; instead, he places his hand on top of mine and squeezes it gently. Electric shockwaves surge through his touch into me, and the rage settles inside me for just a moment. We drive off in silence. Eli is my calm in the severe storm that is brewing.

Once we get back to his place—well, *our* place—I head to my room to start sifting through the folders on the flash drive. Inserting the drive into my laptop, I exhale. Scrolling through the different folders, my eyes land on the one labeled *Gabriella*.

Chapter 4

Beloved Wife

One week before the death of Chance Richardson…

Chance's point of view:

Next Wednesday, I am taking Claudette on a father-daughter date in our old town. I made arrangements with Evi to save our favorite booth. Evi's is a special place for us; it's where I took Claudette after Claudia was called to be with the angels. I can't wait to spend time with my baby girl, my Cheetah. I have missed her so much these past few weeks. It's the longest we've been apart.

My friend Adam is coming over today to conduct a spell so I can speak to my beloved wife while Gabriella and the girls are out shopping. It's time Claudette learned the truth about her heritage and the dangers lurking in the shadows. Mashalville is my home, but the evil that has taken root here must be stopped. Unfortunately, it will be up to Claudette to face this darkness head-on. No teenager should have to carry the burden of the entire town on their shoulders. Still, this is the fate we have been dealt.

There is a knock on the door. I open it, and Adam pushes past me.

"Chance, my man, we have to do this quick. I have a date tonight!" he says, pulling out a candle from his bag.

"Well, we better hurry then. Let's get this done so you can go sweep your lady off her feet."

"Appreciate it, man," Adam chuckles, dashing around the living room and setting everything in place for the spell.

"How has your day been so far?" I ask, making small talk as he prepares for the ritual.

"Today was a nightmare!" Adam screws up his face. "Next week, we have another batch of kids turning seventeen who still need to decide whether they want to become mags or remain a norm. I also need to plan my lessons. And once I leave here, I have to pick up Lin."

Nodding in understanding. "Sounds like a lot on your plate."

Adam half smirks. "You have no idea. It's one thing to deal with teenage hormones. It's another when they choose to keep their magic."

Slapping him on the back. "You handle it like a pro, man. I don't know how you do it, I have three teenage girls, and that's challenging enough."

"No offense, man, but I would never trade places with you."

"None taken. Teenage daughters are a different ball game." I chuckle.

"No arguments there." He says, waving his hand back and forth.

"Also, I wanted to tell you taking in Lin was very noble of you."

He nods. "Yeah, it was the right thing to do after his parents were killed."

"Speaking of that, we need to figure out what happened to all the witches who were murdered."

"I agree." Adam retrieves a piece of paper from his pocket. "Chase, are you ready to get started?"

Nodding my head.

"Recite this spell word for word three times," he instructs, handing me the paper.

Silently reciting the incantation in my head, I nod once more, and Adam lights the candle.

"I am going to fall asleep, and when I do, Claudia will cross over."

"Got it," I reply. "Let's do this."

Adam pauses. "I have one question before we begin: why haven't you tried talking to Claudia before?"

That's a significant question. I was severely depressed after losing the love of my life, and I made the hardest decision to move on for my daughter. I figured it was best to never cross that path of bringing Claudia back. She is no longer in the realm of the living, and I have accepted that. However, our daughter is in danger.

I choose my words carefully. "There is a war brewing amongst the witches, and I need to speak with Claudia."

A crease forms between Adam's brows, and he nods slowly. "I can smell war in the air. There is some deep-rooted dark magic going amuck."

"Agreed," I reply.

"Ready?"

Nodding my head, I recite the spell. "In this sacred hour, I call upon the leader of the Light World to allow me time with Claudia, the one I love and honor," I repeat the spell three times, and Adam falls into a deep slumber.

The lights flicker off and on as a beaming white light fills the room. A brisk wind swirls around, causing goosebumps on my skin, and the air in the room turns cold. I exhale, and I see my breath form a mist. A cloud of smoke appears in front of me, taking the shape of a slim and curvy silhouette. Claudia walks through the smoke, a small smile on her beautiful brown-skinned face. Tears form in my eyes, and I reach for her hand.

"Claudia," I whisper, my voice trembling with emotion.

She squeezes my hand gently. "I'm here," she says, and she falls into my embrace. I hold her as tight as I can, never wanting to let go again. When we finally pull away, I squeeze her shoulders, forearms, and wrists, making sure she is real and not just a figment of my imagination.

Claudia's eyes meet mine. "I'm real, my love."

With her words, I press my lips to hers, savoring the taste of her sweet kiss. She feels cold, but my heart warms at her touch. I have missed my wife, my one true love.

Our lips part, and her brown eyes suddenly turn black before turning brown again.

"What is it?" I ask, running my fingers along her arms and grasping her hands, pulling her close to me.

"We don't have much time, Chance," she says. "And this is a serious matter."

"What do you mean, Claudia? What's going on?"

"There's something I need to tell you. It's about our daughter." Claudia pauses before scolding me. "How could you allow her to move out, Chance?"

Scratching the back of my neck, I look everywhere but at her.

She grabs my chin, forcing me to meet her gaze.

My shoulders slump. "How did you know?"

"Sometimes, I peek through the veil. Imagine my surprise when I saw that she wasn't living with you anymore."

I swallow hard. "Kevin is a fine young man, Claudia. I thought Claudette would be happier living with him instead of living under the same roof with…" I trail off, suddenly feeling awkward discussing my current wife with my dead wife.

Claudia grasps my hands in hers. "I just want you to be happy, Chance. That's all I ever wanted," she says softly. "I am not upset you moved on. I am upset at what it has done to our daughter." There's sadness in her eyes as she speaks. "Kevin is up to no good, Chance. He's not who he says he is. And those twins are not much better. However…" She briefly looks away before continuing. "Gabriella does love you."

Her words hit me like a ton of bricks. "I thought if I kept Claudette here, she would try to—"

"I know," she says, cutting me off. "I was there when she stepped in front of the train." Her voice breaks slightly. "I saved her just in time. But she's hurting, Chance. I will continue to watch over her and protect her, but you need to do your part, too. Which brings me to my next purpose: There has been talking in the Light World that evil is brewing—a much more powerful darkness than what's been going on in this town. This greater evil stems from the Dark World, and our daughter is the key to stopping it. You must get her away from Kevin. He is not right for her, and he is not the one–"

The lights begin flickering off and on, and our eyes lock.

"My time is up, my love." Her body begins to dissolve into a mist, and I reach out to grab her hand one last time. "Please protect our daughter at all costs. Kevin is not her soulmate, Chance. Her soulmate is E–"

She disappears through a cloud of smoke, and Adam wakes up.

"No!" I shout. "Go back under, Adam! I need more time with her!"

But it's too late.

Adam regards me with a solemn expression. "I can't, Chance."

"What do you mean you *can't*?"

"I can't just bring people back from the Light World whenever I want. That's not how it works."

Running my fingers through my hair. "What do we do then?"

Adam pulls out a gold pendant from his bag. There is a small line on the pendant that is drifting in a circle. I survey it closely, however, I can't tell what I am looking at.

"Well?" I ask expectantly.

Adam explains, "I can only bring someone back from the Light World when the veil is open."

"When will the veil be open again?"

Adam sighs. "According to this," he jiggles the pendant, "the next time the veil will be open is next month."

Feeling impatient, I pace back and forth in frustration.

Adam looks at me with a furrowed brow. "What did Claudia say that has you so worried?"

I stop pacing to meet his gaze. "She said not to trust Kevin."

Adam's mouth forms a silent O.

"Claudia mentioned she peeks through the veil sometimes. How does she do that?"

"Chance, peeking through the veil, and stepping through are different things," Adam explains. "Peeking through the veil allows her to see glimpses of the other side without being seen or heard."

Pinching my bottom lip between my index finger and thumb. "How was Claudia able to save Claudette if she couldn't be seen or heard?"

Adam pauses, his brow furrowing in thought. "Have you ever experienced a haunting?"

"No," I reply, folding my arms across my chest.

"It is possible that Claudia blew cold air onto Claudette to give her a sign that she was there, but I don't know, Chance. You would have to ask her."

That is the problem; I can't speak to her again until next month.

"How do you expect to get your love-struck daughter away from Kevin?" Adam raises an eyebrow.

If I push too hard, Claudette will only rebel, and if I'm not careful, I could very well force her into his arms forever. What do I do?

Adam waves his hands in front of my face, taking me out of my inner musing. "Chance, my man, are you okay?"

"No, Adam. I'm not. If Kevin is indeed evil, then that could mean he's caused Earth witches to die. My daughter is in danger."

Adam looks at me with concern, his brow furrowed. "But this has been going on for decades. Kevin hasn't been alive that long."

"True." I need to find a way to subtly guide Claudette without being too forceful. "I am going to compose documents for Claudette and save them on a secure drive. She will have access to the information she needs about this town: magic, her family history, and the dangers."

Adam agrees, nodding silently with approval.

Next week, when Claudette and I meet for our father-daughter date, I will present her with this flash drive, and we will handle the next steps together.

Chapter 5

Claudette's Father

The day of Chance Richardson's death…

Eli's point of view:

"Kevin and his minions are planning something big!" Jeremiah shouts, walking into my bedroom.

My fists clench at my brother's disclosure. "What are you talking about, Jere? What do you know?"

A crease forms between Jeremiah's eyebrows. "I overheard Kevin telling Tanya and Tristan that a plan involving Claudette's father is going down tonight! This is serious, Eli. Kevin has been murdering Earth witches for some time now."

I throw on a jacket and grab my car keys so I can head over to Claudette's father's house to warn him about the danger he may be in. Claudette doesn't believe me when I tell her Kevin can't be trusted; maybe I can convince her father to believe me instead before it's too late.

"Where are you going?" Jeremiah asks.

"To warn Mr. Richardson."

Jeremiah frowns. "What are you going to say to him, Eli? That his daughter's boyfriend is a murderer? He will ask for proof."

My shoulders sag. "Jere, I don't know, but I have to try. I can't just sit back and do nothing. Mr. Richardson is the only family Claudette has left."

Jeremiah's frown deepens. "I don't want Kevin and his minions coming after me next."

"Dude!" I shout, "What do you expect me to do? I love this girl! I can't sit back and let something happen to her father. I promise no one will know I found out from you."

"She is not your girl or your responsibility, Eli. Stay out of it!" Jeremiah retorts, rubbing his temples.

He is right. Claudette is not my girlfriend, and she doesn't feel the same way about me. However, she is my mate, and we are fated to be together. I can't ignore the danger her father is in. I have to do something to help. Until she realizes that she is my destiny, I will love and protect her from the sidelines.

"I have to do something," I tell him firmly.

"Why can't you just let it go?"

Exhaling slowly, I continue, "I can't stand by and do nothing when someone I care about is in trouble. She is my mate."

Jeremiah eyes me warily. "Are you sure she is your soulmate?"

"Yes!" I reply with conviction. "Electric shocks ricocheted from my fingertips to my toes the first time I touched her. We were connected."

Jeremiah looks skeptical, but I can see the wheels turning in his head.

"I will use the moon bracelet to be sure she is my mate."

"Fine," he finally concedes, "the bracelet will confirm your bond." He lets out an exasperated sigh. "Just be careful."

"I will."

"I will text you on my way to the house. Our mother knows that Kevin and his minions are up to something," Jeremiah says.

EARTH

I nod before leaving the room to head to my car.

Sweat is dripping down my temples when I park up in front of Mr. Richardson's house. I grip the steering wheel tight. How do you properly tell a father that his daughter's boyfriend is not who he seems to be? There is no easy way! I will come off as jealous or paranoid, and I am far from either. *This is a messy situation!*

Slouching lower in the driver's seat, I watch Gabriella and the twins leave the house. I wait in my car for them to drive away before mustering up the courage to approach Mr. Richardson. Steadying my breathing, I inhale and exhale once more before finally getting out of the car and walking towards the front door. *Here goes nothing.*

Knocking on the door, I wait for what feels like an eternity before Mr. Richardson answers.

"Hello, Eli," he greets me. "What brings you here today?"

"Hello, Mr. Richardson," I reply nervously. "I wanted to talk to you about something important."

Mr. Richardson nods and gestures for me to trail him inside the house.

Following him into the house to the kitchen, he offers me something to drink, but I politely decline. Kevin and his minions will be here at any moment, and I need to get this off my chest before they arrive.

"What's on your mind, Eli? Claudette should be here soon, so we should make this quick," Mr. Richardson says, looking at his watch.

I get straight to the point.

"I have to talk to you about Kevin," I reply.

Mr. Richardson's eyebrows knit together. "Eli, I do not want to get in the middle of you and Kevin's teenage love quarrel over my daughter."

How did he know?

"Sir, it's not about that; it's about something entirely different," I assure him, swallowing hard before continuing. "I know you are an Earth witch. *Kevin* has been murdering Earth witches to regain his magic."

Mr. Richardson runs a hand through his hair. "That's a serious accusation, Eli. What proof do you have, young man?"

Gulping back the lump in my throat, I answer him truthfully. "I can't give away my source, sir, but this person is credible. I believe Kevin, Tanya, and Tristan are planning something as we speak."

I am interrupted by Mr. Richardson's phone ringing. He raises his index finger to signal for me to wait as he answers the call.

"Hello, Kevin. How are you feeling? Claudette told me you weren't feeling well." Mr. Richardson listens intently, his expression changing as he speaks with Kevin.

Speak of the devil himself!

I start pacing back and forth in the kitchen, waiting for him to finish his call.

He hangs up and turns to me, a serious look on his face, and I immediately stop pacing. "Kevin is on his way here."

My face pales. "Kevin cannot be trusted! Sir! Perhaps I should stay here with you." I try to convince him.

Mr. Richardson shakes his head. "Eli, Kevin doesn't have magic. What can he do to hurt me?"

"You don't have any magic either. Please let me stay." I insist, hoping he will reconsider, but he doesn't.

He reaches for something, a flash drive, from underneath a vase and slides it into his pocket. "I appreciate your concerns, Eli, but I will be fine. Thank you." He looks out of the window and sees Kevin approaching. "Kevin is here to discuss important matters."

That was fast!

I reluctantly turn to leave, heading towards the back door before stopping myself. "Do you believe me?"

He turns back to me, his expression grave. "I believe you, Eli. But we will need credible proof for Claudette to believe us. Trust your instincts to keep her safe, and keep yourself safe as well."

"I will do whatever it takes to protect her." I exit from the back to avoid being seen by Kevin and the two people with him.

Surveying them from my car, I have a clear visual of Kevin and Mr. Richardson talking in the living room. I'm trying to get a closer look at the heavy-set man, or maybe it's a woman, but I can't quite make out their features from this distance. There's another person right behind the robust individual, but their face is obscured by the angle of the window. *I need a closer look!* The only significant thing I can see is something shiny reflecting on the person's left arm. *Maybe a bracelet?* Perhaps it's a woman? I can't really tell from here.

My phone vibrates, and I quickly glance down at the screen to see Claudette calling. I ignore the call and continue to watch Mr. Richardson through the window. I'm on a mission to obtain hard evidence, and I don't want to speak to her until I have concrete proof in hand.

Beep. Who is it now?

Jeremiah:

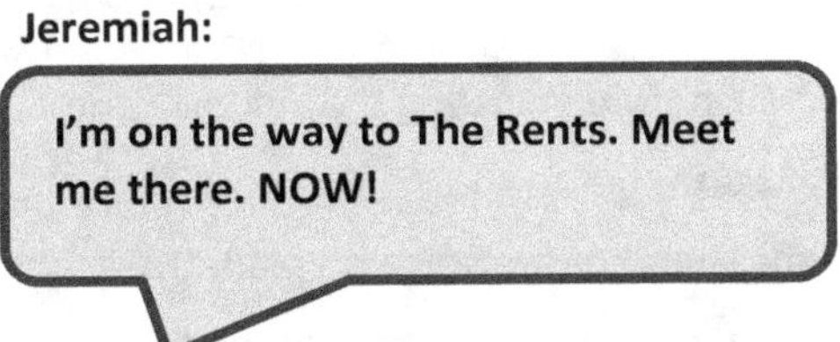

Jeremiah sometimes refers to our parents as *The Rents* because they do not care about us.

I quickly text back and start the ignition. The engine roars and comes to life. Glancing back at the window again, I see Mr. Richardson, Kevin, and the two individuals standing in a circle, talking. With a sigh escaping my lips, I press down on the accelerator and race towards The Rent's house.

It's a twenty-minute drive. Pulling up to the house, I storm into my mother's office. She and my father fear Earth witches and want nothing to do with them. They also knew Kevin had been murdering Earth witches to reclaim his magic all along, and they did nothing about it.

My mother jumps in her seat when I enter. "Eli, what are you doing here?"

"What is Kevin planning?" I shout.

Fidgeting with her 911 machine, my mother rolls her eyes and says nothing.

Slamming my clenched fist on her brown wooden desk. "Answer me!"

"I don't know what he is planning," she shrugs.

Closing my eyes, I focus on my breathing. Because she is my mother, I have a slight respect for her. Still, she is evil, and if it comes down to it, the little respect I have for her will be gone. I stand to my full height and back away from her desk, eyeing her with suspicion.

She hits the top of her machine. "Darn thing work!"

Turning my back to her, I clench my jaw. *What am I going to do?*

Suddenly, a 911 call echoes throughout the room.

"911 What's your emergency?"

Rushing to my mother's desk, I lean in to hear better. "Turn it up a bit!" I shout.

My mother gives me a sharp look before adjusting the volume.

"My father! My father is not breathing!"

A chill slithers up my spine—the sound of the voice is Claudette's!

"Okay, I need you to calm down. Please tell me your name."

No! This is what I was afraid of. Glancing at my watch, it's only been about forty-five minutes since I left Mr. Richardson's house. How could this have happened so soon?

Fists clenched, I march out of my mother's office. This cannot be happening. I just saw Mr. Richardson alive and well with Kevin and two others. Claudette's shrieks echo in my ears, and my heart shatters for her. If her father does not recover, she will be devastated. *If he is not breathing, then he must be dead!* I knew Kevin could not be trusted! *I should have stayed there!*

"Where are you going, Eli?" my mother calls out, following me out of her office.

"I am going to Kevin's house!" I shout back.

"For *what*?"

I freeze in place, my eyes narrowing as I take a moment to observe her carefully. "Kevin killed Mr. Richardson!" *Is she delirious?*

"Eli, you're jumping to conclusions. The dispatcher told Claudette to conduct CPR on her father. You don't know if he is dead." She replies, playing stupid.

"Mother! I know Kevin has been killing Earth witches to regain his magic!"

She appears to be stunned. Jeremiah and my father enter the living room.

Jeremiah shakes his head. "I don't think that's a good idea, Eli." He must keep up pretenses by siding with our parents. As far as they know, we do not get along, which is true in some cases. He is the worst roommate.

"I don't care," I spit through gritted teeth, slamming the door behind me.

I pull up to Kevin's house, overwhelmed with a wrath of fury that has been building inside me for weeks.

Balling up my fist, I bang on the door. Kevin opens it, and I punch him square in the nose, using my magic to close the door behind me.

He stumbles back, grabbing his bloody nose. "What is wrong with you?"

Motioning my hand in a circle, I levitate him off the floor. "You know exactly what you did!" I seethe, hurling him against the ceiling and then throwing him into the wall.

"I know you killed him!" I growl, my eyes glowing with anger, as I watch

Kevin struggle to stand up.

He charges at me, and we go blow for blow. He uppercuts me in the chin, causing my teeth to collide painfully. I shake it off and counter with a right hook to his jaw and a left jab to his ribs. He staggers back but then regains his footing and retaliates with a swift punch to my stomach. The pain shoots through me, but I refuse to back down. Pushing forward, I tackle him to the floor, pinning him beneath me and throwing a series of punches to his face until he is bleeding profusely.

"I know you killed Claudette's father!"

He spits out blood and smirks, confirming my suspicions with a sinister laugh. "Oh, is he dead?"

This sick demon is proud!

"You're a monster," I growl, tightening my grip on him. "You'll pay for what you've done." I shove him back on the floor and stand up.

"Dude, are you upset because I got the girl and you didn't?" Kevin taunts, trying to get under my skin. He gets up and wipes the blood from his face, a cocky grin on his lips.

Taking a deep breath, I try to control my rage before doing something I'll regret.

He walks towards me, poking me in the chest with his finger. "Is it because Claudette trusts me more than she trusts you? Looks like you never had a chance."

Trying to maintain my composure, I feel my fists tighten.

"Or is it because I got to be inside her?" He scoffs, a smug expression on his face. "Grinding my length into her uncharted territory until she screamed my name, her body writhing beneath me in pleasure. You'll never know that feeling, will you?"

My vision blurs with rage. The thought of him touching her makes my blood run cold, and I resist the urge to lunge at him as he licks his lips, reminiscing about taking her innocence.

"You're disgusting!" I spit out.

Kevin blows on his fingernails and rubs them against his shirt, a sadistic smirk playing on his lips. "Jealousy is an ugly look on you, Eli. But hey, I can't blame you for wanting what I have." His words cut through me like a knife. "The little slut was worth it. Especially because I had her first!"

Clenching my jaw, the urge to make him pay for his words grows stronger with each passing moment.

"Imagine if I had trapped her!" he laughs.

Balling my fist, I bite back on the urge to punch him in the face for his callous words.

Kevin laughs again when he sees my clenched fist. "Don't worry, I will use protection when I have fun with her again," he says with a smirk. "You know I can have her anytime I want. I have her wrapped around my finger."

His arrogance and disrespect for her make the anger inside me boil over, and I can't hold back any longer as I lunge towards him in a fit of rage.

Grabbing him by his shirt. "You're a disgusting excuse for a human being," I seethe. "She deserves better than you."

I was supposed to be her first. Not him! She fell in love with his charm and manipulation.

Despite my outburst, he maintains a smug smirk on his face. "You wish you had her first, but I beat you to it." He laughs in my face, sealing the nail in his own coffin.

His words only fuel my fury. I don't know how Claudette trusted this demon of a man, and she still doesn't see his true colors. I need solid proof.

Letting my temper consume me, I knock him unconscious with a swift punch to the jaw. That was for taking my soulmate from me.

I will prove to Claudette that he is not the man she thinks he is, no matter what it takes!

Chapter 6

The Gabriella Files

Clicking on the folder labeled *Gabriella*, I scroll through the contents. She was born and raised in Mashalville as a Moon witch. On her seventeenth birthday, she decided to keep her magic, but she fell for a guy who chose to be a norm. She thought they were in love until he knocked her up with the demon twins after her seventeenth birthday. He disappeared from town shortly after, leaving Gabriella pregnant and alone. Embarrassed and devastated, she fled Mashalville the day after the twins' first birthday to find him. *Interesting.*

Scrolling further, I continue reading about the twins' father and when Gabriella tracked him down, only to discover that he had a new family. I stop at a picture of the twin's father with his other family, smiling and happy. There are multiple pictures of him with his new wife and children, clearly showing the life he chose over Gabriella and their twins. *Wow! What a prick!* Zooming in on the photo of his daughter, I find it uncanny how much she and I favor one another. *Perhaps this is why the twins hate me so much.* Resting my forehead on my palm, I shake my head. I wonder if the twins know about their half-siblings. *They have to, right?* Because why else would they be so cruel to me? I look just like their half-sister! Still, it doesn't excuse their behavior toward me. It's not my fault their father chose to start a new family.

Exiting the folder, I click on Gabriella's parents' folder. Her mother passed away after she gave birth to her, leaving her father to raise her alone. She had no siblings, and her father died from an aneurysm a few years after she left town. *What a life! I actually feel sorry for her.*

She clearly had no intentions of moving back to Mashalville; there was nothing left for her here. Perhaps she does–*did* love my father.

Exiting out of Gabriella's folder, I go back into my dad's; he has the most subfolders under his name. The one that sparks my interest is labeled *Claudette*. Clicking on it, a letter from him pops up, dating back to the last week he was alive.

Dear Claudette,

If you are reading this, it means I am no longer with you, and I am so sorry for leaving you alone, Cheetah. I love you more than words can express, and I hope you can find happiness without me. Please know that I did the best I could and did what I thought was best for you. I am sorry I fell in love with Gabriella, but she fulfilled something in me that I couldn't explain to you at the time. I was lonely when your mother died, and I felt overwhelmed with depression. Your mother was my one true love, and I wanted nothing more than to be with her again. Still, I knew I couldn't leave you behind.

When you were a little girl, you asked me what happened to your mom. I didn't know how to explain it to you in a way that wouldn't hurt you, so I hid in my office and avoided the conversation. My pain was something I carried alone, but I shouldn't have hidden it from you. I knew you were grieving, too, and we should have been mourning together. It was selfish of me to keep my pain from you. Please forgive me.

When I met Gabriella, she made me feel complete again, and I fell for her. I am sorry she didn't treat you the way your mom would have, and there is nothing I can say that would make any of this better. I was a fool. Although you and Gabriella didn't get along, if there was one thing I knew, she did love me and care for you. Because of that love, she moved back to Mashalville to face the council. They wouldn't have found her as long as she didn't practice magic, and she forbade the twins from using their magic as well. Still, she chose to come back for me. I was the one who wanted to come back to this town so you could learn about your magical heritage and make your decision on your seventeenth birthday. I never imagined it would lead to this. There is so much more I wish I could have told you, guided you, and prepared you for. But I left this flash drive with all the information you need to navigate this world on your own.

You will need our family's Earth book. It is hidden in a locked box under the floorboard underneath your bed in your room. The combination is 3-2-1-7, and the key you will need is in my Earth necklace. Ask Gabriella for it; she knows I left it for you. If, by chance, the box has been removed from the floorboard underneath your bed, you can use my ring to locate it. Please be safe, and remember that you are never truly alone. You can seek help from Jimmy from the council and Adam Goatfair. They will have more information on keeping you safe!

Your mother and I will always be watching over you, no matter where you are.

I love you, Cheetah.

Love, Dad.

My eyes swell with tears as I read my father's final words. I sob, clutching my chest at the weight of his absence. My father was stupid and in love, but he always cared deeply for my safety and loved me unconditionally. *His necklace?* I wipe the tears from my eyes and the snot from my nose. *My father's necklace and ring are missing!* Thinking back to the day my dad died, I remember he wasn't wearing either. *Did someone take them?*

My phone rings, and Kevin's name flashes across my screen. *What does he want?* Nevertheless, I answer anyway.

Me: Hello.

Kevin: Hey, babe.

Me: I'm sorry. Babe?

Kevin: Claudette, I don't want to fight with you anymore. I think we should make up.

Me: Funny. I think we should break up. What do you want, Kevin?

Kevin: We're just going through a rough patch—nothing serious. Or are you already with Eli?

Me: What? I am not with Eli. We are just friends.

Kevin: Sure, sure. I thought you should know that you can't trust your friend.

Me: What is it with you and Eli singing the same tune?

Kevin: Trust me, this is not fun for me either. Eli's parents are plotting to kill you. I thought maybe you should know.

Me: Trust you? Not anymore. Thank you for warning me of my planned demise, though.

Hanging up on him, I sigh, tossing my phone onto the bed. Eli's parents are plotting to kill me? That's a new one. I'll have to confront Eli about this and get to the bottom of it. Storming out of my room, I stomp down the hallway to Eli's room. I barge in without knocking first and find Eli walking out of the bathroom, a towel wrapped around his waist.

We both freeze, our eyes locking in surprise, and his towel drops to the floor, exposing his length to me.

Woah!

Eli pulls his towel back up quickly, his cheeks flushing, and I cover my eyes with my hands.

"Have you heard of knocking, Claudette?"

My face grows hot. *I'm so embarrassed.*

"I am so sorry for barging in like that, Eli. I just wanted to talk to you about something important." I peek through my fingers to check if he is decent before continuing the conversation.

"What is so important that you couldn't knock first?" Eli presses with a hint of teasing in his voice.

"I promise I'll knock next time," I say sheepishly.

Eli cocks an eyebrow, looking at me.

"Kevin called me."

His jaw clenches. "Let me get dressed. I'll meet you in the living room."

With a nod, I quickly sprint out of his room, a small smile playing on my lips as I savor the memory of what I had just witnessed.

I wait for Eli on the sofa and daydream about him throwing me over his shoulder and carrying me back to his r–

"What did Kevin want?" Eli appears, sitting beside me, his expression unreadable.

I bite my bottom lip. He looks so handsome and distracting that I almost forget about Kevin's call.

"Hello, Claudette," he says, snapping his fingers in front of my face.

He can–

"Claudette!" He raises his voice a little louder this time, snapping me out of my inappropriate daydreaming.

I jump, a blush creeping up on my cheeks. "Sorry, Eli, something… distracted me for a moment."

He gives me a strange look before turning his attention back to the conversation at hand. "What did Kevin want?"

He probably thinks I am crazy. *Maybe I am!*

Shaking my head, I try to focus on Eli's question. "He said your parents want to kill me."

Eli's face is grim. "I see. Kevin should tell my parents they will have to go through me first if they want to get to you."

Wow! Eli would go against his parents for me? *Is it hot in here, or is it just me?*

My cheeks flush as I meet his intense gaze. "Thank you, Eli. That means a lot to me."

He stands up, scratching the back of his neck. *What did I say to make him so nervous?*

Clearing his throat. "I have to show you something."

He disappears from the room, leaving me with a million questions swirling in my head. When he returns, he's holding a candle and a royal blue and gold book with a crescent engraving on the cover. He flips through the pages and stops on a page with a crescent and an Earth symbol overlapping one another. He lights the candle and closes his eyes.

His facial expression is stern and focused. "I call upon the Moon and Earth to access their power, combine our magic, and give us what my heart desires." He repeats this incantation two times.

"What are you doing, Eli?"

"Do you trust me?"

I nod without hesitation.

He shoves his hand in his pocket and pulls out a moon bracelet. "May I?" He asks, holding out the bracelet to my left wrist.

I extend my arm, allowing him to clasp it on.

"Let's see if this works," he says with a determined look in his eyes, and he recites the spell two more times.

"Don't resist, Claudette," he urges.

I do not understand what he is trying to do.

He grabs my hands, and electricity flows between us. I feel complete. Eli recites the spell once more, and we spin in a circle, levitating to the ceiling.

Blue, gold, and brown swirls of light circle us. The papers in the living room fly around us like a tornado, and visions—or perhaps memories, *Eli's memories*—flash before my eyes. *I can see everything he has seen!*

Eli was at my house the day my father died, and so was Kevin. Two other people came with Kevin. Eli confronts Kevin at his house. His reaction to Eli's accusation is suspicious. He may not have killed my father, but he knows who did! The boys fight. Kevin taunts Eli; he calls me a *slut!* Eli knocks him out.

How could I be so stupid?

Kevin doesn't love me!

He never loved me.

He used me. And he acted as an accomplice to my father's murder.

He lied to me.

Manipulated me.

I trusted him.

My heart shatters into a million pieces, equivalent to Kevin piercing his hand through my chest and ripping out my heart, squeezing it until it's nothing but a bloody mess.

Letting go of Eli's hands, we drop to the floor abruptly.

"Kevin knows who killed my father?" It comes out as a question, but I already know the answer, and the look on Eli's face confirms it.

Kevin's betrayal cuts deeper than I ever thought possible. He was so good at lying and pretending to care. He strung me along, toying with my feelings, all while plotting behind my back. He is so deceitful. A master manipulator. A wolf in sheep's clothing. I never saw it coming. But Eli did, and he tried to warn me so many times. I should have listened to him. He has been there for me since the beginning, trying to get me to see the truth about Kevin. He even beat Kevin up for me. He was right about him the whole time.

I cup Eli's face in my hands, pulling him close to me. "Thank you for always looking out for me," I whisper before pressing my lips against his in a long, overdue kiss. I try to express my gratitude for his loyalty and protection in a way that words cannot fully convey in this kiss. He responds by wrapping his arms around me tight, pulling me even closer as if to say that he will always be there for me no matter what.

The worst kinds of people are the ones who pretend to care about you but then turn around and stab you in the back. Their loyalty is shallow and self-serving, and they only support you when it's beneficial for them. As soon as you no longer serve their interests, they will abandon you. Kevin is the epitome of betrayal and selfishness—he got what he wanted from me and then discarded me like I was nothing.

Eli and I reluctantly pull away. The pain in his eyes is evident, mirroring the hurt I feel in my own heart.

"Did you see the two people who came with Kevin?"

Replaying Eli's memories in my head, it's hard to distinguish who they were. One of them had curves, implicating she was a woman, while the other had none, suggesting he was a man. *Who are they?*

"Yes, it was a man and a woman." Recalling the truth serum I used on Kevin, I say, "I asked Kevin if he knew who killed my father. He said no. But he hesitated when he responded."

"Yes, Claudette! He hesitated because he was lying. He's been lying to you the entire time. You finally believe me now."

Nodding my head, I finally believe Eli for the first time about Kevin's deceitful nature. Turning away from him, I walk to my room, with Eli following closely behind me. I grab my phone to block and delete Kevin's number; I want nothing to do with him anymore! Falling to the floor—I had been blind for too long—sobbing as I think back to the night I lost my virginity to Kevin.

With Eli, my knight in shining armor, kneeling beside me, his embrace envelops me, making me feel loved and cherished.

"Kevin told me we were fated to be together." I sniffle in between sobs.

Eli wipes my tears away, but despite his best efforts, more tears continue to fall.

"It's going to be okay, Claudette." Eli soothes. "Kevin was wrong about a lot of things. *We're* fated to be together, not you and him. I love you. I have loved you from the first day we touched, and the shockwaves flowed through us. Trust the magic, Claudette. The spell wouldn't have worked if we weren't destined to be together." With tears blurring my vision, I lock eyes with Eli, and his sincere gaze pierces through me. Since the very first day we met, I have felt an undeniable connection with Eli, as if our souls were meant to intertwine.

How could I be so blind not to see the truth in front of me all along?

It was always Eli. *Not* Kevin.

Still, am I ready to admit that out loud to him?

Welcome to the West Side

Classes for "The mags"

- History of Magic—Taught by Mr. Goatfair
Where do Sun, Moon, and Earth witches come from?
- Potion Measurements—Taught by Ms. Caron
The right ingredients to use in a potion.
- Magical Elements—Taught by Mr. Max
How to harness your powers from the Sun, Moon, or Earth.
- Advanced Practical Magic—Taught by Ms. Billie
Spells, potions, and all things magic.

Chapter 7

Back to School

Eli stayed the entire night in my room, comforting me while I sobbed. My father's death broke me, but this was something different, almost sinister.

I trusted Kevin.

I thought he cared for me.

I thought he loved me.

How could I have been so wrong? He tarnished my virtue and broke my heart into tiny pieces. This pain is different. Is this what it feels like to have your heart broken by love? I wouldn't say I like it. I'm only seventeen, yet I thought what Kevin and I had was real and that we would last *forever*. He was my boyfriend, pretending to care for me when, in reality, he didn't. How could anyone be so cruel–so *evil*?

Eli rolls over to face me and flashes me a warm smile. *I wish I had met him first!*

Meeting his gaze, I try to smile back, but the pain in my heart is still fresh. Pools of tears spill down my cheeks again, and Eli gently wipes them away with his thumb.

We have school today, and I am supposed to be getting ready. How do I face Kevin, or anyone else, for that matter? I threatened the entire town, so

I'm not the most likable person right now. And Kevin is living his best life as if nothing happened while I am left to pick up the pieces of my shattered heart. The thought of seeing him again makes me sick to my stomach.

You will get through this! My inner voice assures me.

Sucking in a sharp breath, I wave my hand at the lamp on my nightstand, tossing it to the floor—the shards of glass scatter across the surface.

"Ahh!"

Eli pulls me into his arms, holding me tight. "It's okay to be angry."

I bury my face in his chest, letting out a muffled sob.

How didn't I see this before? The entire time Eli's been in my life, he's been the one holding me together. We had a connection before and after we accepted our magic, and our attraction is undeniable. I should have trusted him sooner, but this was a lesson I needed to learn. I don't know why my life is filled with so much chaos, but there has to be a reason for it all—a silver lining to all this mess, right?

Eli plants a soft kiss on my forehead. "Let's get ready for school. We can face the madness together."

He is right. No matter how much I don't want to go to school today because of the possibility of running into Kevin, I have to rip off the band-aid.

The first two periods go smoothly. I manage to avoid Kevin altogether. Despite not seeing him, my stomach remains twisted in knots as I anticipate the unavoidable confrontation with him. I want to punch him square in the face for what he did. I should tell him I thought about Eli when we were having sex, to see the look on his arrogant face! It probably wouldn't bother him, seeing how he never cared about me in the first place. I roll my eyes at the thought of his indifference. I really need to get rid of this hatred toward him, but he knows who killed my father, and I can't let that go. *I hate him!*

Walking into class, I attempt to turn my frown upside down with a slight smile. Today, we are learning the history of the Sun, Moon, and Earth witches. This should be interesting. In a hurry, Mr. Goatfair strides into the classroom and drops all of his papers on the floor when our gazes meet. He rushes to pick them up. My father mentioned him in his letter. *I should reach out to him soon.*

"Do you need any help with that, Mr. Goatfair?" Isabel offers.

"Yes, thank you, Isabel."

When Mr. Goatfair settles in, he faces us to begin his lesson. "Alright, class, today we will discuss the first two witches." He turns to the board and draws two stick figures to represent the witches.

Leaning toward Isabel, I whisper to her. "Is he seriously drawing stick figures?"

She snorts, trying to stifle a laugh, which causes me to giggle as well.

Mr. Goatfair turns around, shooting us disapproving glances. "Pay attention, you two!"

He faces the board again, continuing his lesson by drawing another stick figure and naming it Mother. Mr. Goatfair walks over to his desk and takes out his pointer.

Clearing his throat. "One thousand years ago, there were two brothers who were gravely ill." He says, pointing to each stick figure on the board. "Their mother cast a dark spell to heal them and granted them gifts. They soon became powerful brothers who couldn't have been more different from one another." He clears his throat once again and looks at each of us. "As they grew older, one turned toward evil, and the other turned toward good. Antus was the evil brother and wanted to become a god to all and rule the world, whereas Jaju just wanted to live in peace. The two disagreed on their purpose. Jaju desired a world for witches to reside in, while Antus aimed to live in the real world and dominate it. After years of resentment, fights, and exposure to humans, Jaju created Jajuville, the Magical Realm, and he gifted his people magic from Fire and Ice. In doing so, he trapped Antus and his followers in a town cloaked by magic and named it Mashalville. Antus became a problem and wanted to perform rituals to sacrifice witches for his personal needs." Mr. Goatfair has the class's undivided attention as he recounts the origin of our magic. He pauses for dramatic effect and then continues. "The witches grew tired of his behavior and stood together, killing him once and for all and banishing him to the Shadow World. Antus was angry and cursed the Sun, Moon, and Earth witches so that every child born from the same coven would be evil and bound to him." He pauses once again and meets my gaze. "When Antus placed his curse on the witches that stood against him, every child born from the same coven was forced to serve him, carrying out his tasks and granting him the ability to reach not only this realm but the Magical Realm."

Listening to Mr. Goatfair's lecture, I find myself leaning into my desk, fully engrossed in his words.

"It is said that Antus created a Shadow King—unbeknownst to Jaju—that is currently wreaking havoc on Jajuville. They will need help preventing an all-out magical war. Only the most powerful witches will prevent this," he says, glancing in my direction.

Why is he looking at me? The bell rings, and shuffling fills the room as everyone gathers their things to leave.

Mr. Goatfair's eyes bore into mine with an intense gaze. "Please read over chapters one through five for tomorrow." He says, still holding my gaze.

I break eye contact first and quickly pack up my things.

"Why was Mr. Goatfair looking at you like that?" Isabel asks as we exit the classroom.

Shrugging my shoulders. "I have no idea."

"That was so weird. It's like he was only talking to you."

Nodding. "I agree, it was weird."

I wonder why he was looking at me when he mentioned Jajuville? My dad left me a lot of helpful information on that flash drive. I'm sure there is something about Jajuville on there. Suddenly, my mind falls on Kevin, and I think about how he was born from the same coven. Eli was right about this, as well. *Kevin probably serves Antus.*

EARTH

I practically jog down the opposite hallway to my next class in an attempt to avoid running into Kevin. Heading to the back of the classroom, I take my seat.

Mr. Max walks in on high alert. "Hello, class. We are going to discuss magical elements today."

Everyone settles into their seats, and I quickly pull out my notebook and pen to take notes.

"As you know, there are Sun, Moon, and Earth witches," Mr. Max begins. "Sun witches harness power from the sun, Moon from the moon, and Earth witches are the most powerful, as they can draw power from all elements of nature on Earth. Today, we are going to focus on Earth magic." He explains, glaring in my direction.

Swallowing the knot forming in my throat, I let out a loud gulp.

"Claudette, would you like to help me teach this lesson?" he asks, his eyes fixed on me.

Why are all my teachers picking on me today?

Not really! "Sure, Mr. Max," I say instead.

He claps his hands together. "Excellent! Earth is an important magical element. There are a few others, such as fire, ice, and water, but our focus today is on Earth and how it pertains to Earth witches."

He gives me a small smile. "Claudette, as an Earth witch, you can use your gift at any time of the day; you can focus on grass, dirt, and trees and let them consume you to harness your power. But if you don't know what you're doing, the magic can drain you. Let me show you."

The classroom illuminates as he opens and closes his hands, causing his eyes to glow a vibrant yellow. Through the window, the sun's rays pour in, creating a fleeting burst of light in his hand before disappearing in an instant.

My face lights up with excitement, and my heart races. *Wow!*

He gives me a reassuring nod. "Go ahead and try it."

Taking a deep breath, I close my eyes and let my senses take over. The floor beneath my feet vibrates, and a warm sensation overrides my body. Flashes of Kevin seize my mind, and I lose control, causing the classroom to shake.

Mr. Max grabs my arm, trying to prevent me from causing destruction. "Claudette, you need to channel the good, not the bad."

My heart beats rapidly beneath my chest as though I were running a marathon, resulting in my abrupt collapse onto the floor.

Mr. Max and the rest of the class gather around me, their faces showing signs of distress.

"Claudette, are you okay?" Mr. Max asks.

"Y—yes, I think so. What happened?" I ask, sitting up and scratching the top of my head.

Mr. Max helps me up. "Claudette, may I ask what you were thinking about?"

Sighing heavily. "I really don't want to talk about it, Mr. Max."

He lowers his gaze. "Maybe we can go over accessing your power in a more positive way. Whatever you were thinking about caused your powers to overload."

Nodding in understanding, I smile. "Yes, of course."

"Try again," he suggests.

Inhaling deeply, I concentrate on channeling my magic. As I sway my hand back and forth over my feet, I feel the floor trembling beneath me and the tiles gradually unfolding, revealing a gaping hole that descends into the ground. The dirt emerges from the depths of the hole, swirling in the palm of my hand. A smile forms on Mr. Max's lips as the class collectively gasps.

"See what you can do when you focus on the good?"

Smiling from ear to ear, I hold the dirt in my hand and use my other hand to spin it in a circle—like a mini tornado. The class watches as I push forward, returning the dirt back to the Earth and closing the hole in the middle of the classroom floor. The bell rings, and Mr. Max shouts over his shoulder to read over chapter ten for tomorrow's quiz. Nodding, I grab my bag and pack up my books before hurrying out of the classroom. My next class is my favorite, Potion Measurements. Today, we are learning how to create a healing potion.

Chapter 8

Rage

Once again, I make my way to class avoiding a certain *someone*. Entering the classroom, I proceed to my desk in the middle of the room, next to Eli. A charming smile crosses his face when our eyes meet.

"Hey," he greets, nudging my hip with his elbow. "How has your day been so far?"

Removing my bag from my shoulder, I hang it on the back of my chair. A sigh escapes my lips when I lower myself in my seat, shooting him a disapproving glare.

Eli chuckles. "What's all that for?"

"I have been trying to avoid you know who, like my life depends on it all day."

He briefly looks away, his jaw clenching and unclenching, before meeting my gaze again. "Claudette, you're eventually going to have to face him, and when you do, I will be there for you."

Rising from my seat, I throw my arms around his neck to hug him tight. "Thank you," I whisper.

"Of course," he murmurs.

I pull away and settle back into my chair when Ms. Caron strides into the classroom.

"Hello, class! Are you all ready for today's lesson?" She asks with a wide grin on her face.

The class nods with enthusiasm.

"Okay, let's get started. Who would like to help me hand out the tools and ingredients for today's lesson?" she asks, glancing around the classroom.

Raising my hand. "I would like to help," I volunteer.

Ms. Caron gives me a wink, and I head to the front of the room.

"We are going to hand out vials for the potions, mini cauldrons, hot plates, a needle, and measuring cups." She meticulously hands me each object, making sure they are transferred to me with the utmost care.

I carefully take each item and distribute it to my classmates.

After depositing the tools required for the potion, she hands me the necessary ingredients: a cup of water, ginger powder, and elderberry juice.

Taking my seat, I place the items in front of me. Ms. Caron, in an effort to capture our attention, clears her throat and proceeds to provide step-by-step instructions.

She walks to the board and writes *Healing Potion*.

"I need everyone's undivided attention because we will be using hot plates today. Please place your cauldrons on the hot plate." She waits until everyone has followed her instructions before continuing. "Next, I want you to open the package that has a needle in it and poke yourself."

Everyone exchanges uneasy glances, and whispers fill the classroom.

She claps her hands together. "Settle down, settle down. The needle is just for pricking your finger to add droplets of your blood to the potion. It's completely safe and necessary for the Healing Potion to work." Ms. Caron waits for the chitter chat to simmer down, and then she continues. "Use the needle to prick your finger and add three drops of blood to the cauldron. When you are finished, please pour one cup of water and one-third cup of ginger powder." She pauses for a moment, eyeing the class warily. "If you were making this potion at home, you would use fresh ginger and grind it into powder. However, we have limited time. Do you guys know what ginger is good for in terms of healing properties?" She asks.

"Ginger has potent anti-inflammatory and antioxidant properties." A student answers from the front of the classroom.

"Correct, and it's also good for relieving nausea, improving the immune system, brain function, cholesterol, and weight loss, amongst other things." She says with a smile. "See how it is bubbling? Now add two-thirds cup of elderberry juice. Elderberry is important for its health-promoting properties. Get to stirring." She instructs, letting out one of her usual loud cackles. Ms. Caron enjoys mixing and stirring together potions. "Let it cool for about three minutes, and then I need a volunteer," she says.

"I'll do it," Destiny says, walking to the front of the class.

"Excellent!" Ms. Caron exclaims. She gestures her hand forward and back, and a dagger appears.

Destiny bravely places her hand in Ms. Caron's hand. Ms. Caron slices it. She then pours the potion on the wound, and within five minutes, the gash disappears.

Gasps echo throughout the room.

Ms. Caron grins from ear to ear, showcasing Destiny's healed hand before us. "Voilà," she beams. "Now you all try it."

Leaning over to Eli, I whisper, "I am not cutting myself to see if this potion works."

Eli lets out a small chuckle, shaking his head. He materializes a dagger and slices his hand.

My eyes are as wide as a saucer. "What are you doing?"

"She told us to try it out for ourselves. I want to see if the potion works." He raises an eyebrow at me to follow suit as he pours his potion into the wound.

I watch in horror as Eli's cut miraculously heals before my eyes.

Ms. Caron walks by each desk, observing everyone's progress and nodding her head in approval. When she reaches my desk, she folds her arms across her chest.

Understanding the hint, I materialize a dagger from thin air and slice my hand. "Ouch!" I wince in pain as blood starts pooling on the desk. *Perhaps I cut myself too deeply.*

Ms. Caron's and Eli's eyes are wide.

"Hurry and pour the potion on your hand," Eli urges me.

"Oh, right!" I reply, pouring it on my cut.

The wound heals, and Ms. Caron regards me with a satisfied grin.

Examining the front and back of my hand in awe, I'm amazed. The cut is gone, with not even a scar left behind. *Magic is amazing!*

The bell rings and we gather our things to head to our next class. Isabel, Destiny, and Lin join Eli and me as we stride down the hallway. My anxiety resurfaces from the anticipation of running into Kevin, and Eli notices the look of distress on my face. He pulls me to the side, and Isabel, Destiny, and Lin exchange concerned glances.

Isabel stands beside me, her long lashes fluttering. "Are you okay?"

My mind spirals. Everything Eli said to me was the truth, and Kevin has been lying to me for months.

How can I trust my own judgment?

"Everything Eli said about Kevin is true," I reply.

Isabel glances between Eli and me. "I'm sorry, Claudette. I wanted to tell you," she says.

A slight sense of guilt reflects in Destiny and Lin's eyes as they both turn their gaze elsewhere.

Leaning against the locker. "I don't understand. If everyone knows Kevin is evil, why is he allowed in school? In this town?"

Eli shakes his head, and Isabel replies. "The Witch Council."

My brows pull together, and I screw up my face. "How can a town full of powerful witches allow a teenager to be in control? It makes no sense to me."

Nothing in this town does!

"We don't have solid proof that Kevin is evil," Eli explains. "He appears to be a normal teenager with no magic. His parents told the council that his powers were taken away from him, so he didn't have to make the choice. It was made for him."

"And because he didn't choose, he is not deemed evil," Destiny adds.

"Mr. Goatfair said in class today that Antus cursed the witches of this town," I retort, confused by the town's decision-making process.

"Yes, that is true, according to the history book. However, Kevin's parents believe they found a loophole by taking his magic away before he could make the decision. They thought this would prevent him from becoming evil." Lin chimes in.

Rolling my eyes so far back in my head. "This town is full of idiots!" I mutter under my breath.

The next bell rings and we continue on our way down the hall. Before I get a chance to walk through the doors, I freeze, and an uneasy feeling settles in the pit of my stomach. *Kevin.* He is standing in front of us with his trusted minions behind him, wearing a smug smirk on his face.

He cocks his head to the side. "Hello, Claudette. You haven't returned any of my calls or texts."

Isabel attempts to grab my hand, but I pull away from her.

"I blocked and deleted your number," I say, meeting his gaze head-on.

He takes a step closer to me, feigning innocence. "I'm heartbroken."

"Quit the act, Kevin. You need to have a heart to be heartbroken," I retort.

Kevin's smirk widens.

My stomach churns in disgust. Who is this person before me?

I do not know him anymore.

I guess I never did.

Eli steps in between us, blocking Kevin from getting any closer. "That's enough, Kevin. Leave her alone," he says.

Kevin chuckles. "Are you her knight in shining armor now, Eli?"

Eli's jaw tightens, his eyes narrowing. "I'm just a friend who knows when to step in."

Rolling my eyes. "That's enough." Pushing past Eli to confront Kevin face-to-face. "Who killed my father?"

He grins, crossing his arms and not bothering to respond.

The look on his face is familiar. It has been there all along. I was just too blinded by his good looks and charm—until now. I see the truth in his cold, calculating eyes. *He is pure evil.*

Blackness clouds my vision as anger takes over. I levitate, opening and closing my fist. Kevin falls to his knees and holds his head in agony. I'm causing the veins in his brain to rupture.

"Tell me who killed my father!"

Eli, Isabel, Destiny, and Lin stand frozen in shock. Tanya, Tristan, and the demon twins rush to Kevin's rescue as I give him an aneurysm. *I see the twins have healed themselves.* They attack me with their magic, but it has no effect on me. Opening and closing my fist, they fall to their knees, grabbing their heads. I give them aneurysms as well.

"Claudette, please stop!" Isabel pleads over their agonizing screams.

"Please, Claudette! This isn't you!" Eli shouts.

Ignoring them both, I will not stop until all of them are dead. My rage is consuming me, and the school is shaking, sending everyone panicking and scrambling for safety.

My friends are desperately calling out to me, begging me to take control of my emotions, but I ignore their feeble pleas. My mind is focused on killing those who have caused me so much pain. My magic is powerful, but it is draining me.

Just hold on a little longer until all of them are dead!

Suddenly, Mr. Goatfair, Mr. Max, and Lin hold out an unfamiliar object before me, and they recite a spell that knocks me to the floor. Kevin and his minions collapse as well, relieved. The moment Eli holds my hand, his magic courses through me, easing my anxiety and restoring a sense of peace.

How did they stop me? What was that object they were holding? *Mr. Goatfair must be an Earth witch!* Why else would my father tell me to reach out to him for help? As our eyes meet, he nods with a knowing look as if he can read my thoughts.

Principal Deanwall charges at me, brows knitted together. "My office. Now!" He roars. "Everyone else, go to your next class immediately!"

He storms off in the direction of his office while Eli helps me up. "I'm coming with you."

I hold Eli's arm as we follow Principal Deanwall to his office.

Slamming his door shut behind us, Principal Deanwall whirls around to face me with a look of pure fury. "Miss Richardson, no killing is allowed in this school! Your behavior is unacceptable and will not be tolerated. I am going to have to expel you."

I blink. Once. Twice. Three times. "You can't be serious. Kevin knows who murdered my father. He is evil. And I'm getting expelled? What is wrong with this town?" I spit out.

"Violence is never the answer, Miss Richardson. You need to leave the premises immediately."

"With pleasure," I retort, grabbing my backpack and storming out of the office.

Eli catches up to me in the hallway, and we walk in silence to my locker. I practice my breathing, counting to ten in my head, and swing my hands in circles, bringing my hands together for a single *clap*. All the lockers burst open simultaneously, and books and papers fly out, scattering across the hallway.

Feeling faint and lightheaded, I slightly lose my balance. Eli catches me, a look of concern etched in his deep brown eyes.

"Are you okay?" he asks, steadying me.

Nodding, I glance around the hallway. It looks like a category-three hurricane named St. Claudette has hit Mashal High.

Chapter 9

Hometown

Blinking twice, I see Eli standing tall with his arms crossed over his chest, looking down at me. His expression is unreadable. I have been cooped up in my room since yesterday's incident.

"Get dressed," he instructs, leaving me alone in the room.

Sitting up and rubbing my eyes, I furrow my brows. Why is he telling me to get dressed? The school expelled me. Where is he taking me? Nonetheless, I quickly shower and change into denim high-waisted skinny jeans and a leopard crop top, finishing my look with red slides. I give myself a quick once-over in the mirror and apply my L'Oréal Infallible matte lipstick before heading out to meet Eli in the kitchen.

Eli looks at me, his lips twisting into a sexy smile, and my stomach flips a little. He hands me an everything bagel with cream cheese. *My favorite.*

"We are going to visit your friends today," he says while I bite into the bagel.

"What do you mean?" I ask in between bites.

Eli wipes the cream cheese off the corner of my mouth with his thumb and licks it off. *That was so sexy.*

"I thought it would be nice for you to spend some time with Nicolette,

Spencer, and Mitch, so Lin and I are taking you to your old town."

What?

A huge, goofy grin spreads across my face. "Are you serious?!"

He smiles and nods. "I thought it would be a nice surprise for you."

Excitement bubbles up inside me. "What about Destiny and Isabel?"

Eli chuckles before saying, "Unfortunately, being the principal's daughter has its downsides, and being the girlfriend of the principal's daughter means Isabel has to stay behind for this one."

I am not Principal Deanwall's favorite student at the moment, so it's probably best if they stay put. Eli and Lin are cutting school to take me; Principal Deanwall wouldn't be too pleased if he found out about Destiny and Isabel joining us.

Suddenly, images of yesterday flash through my mind, and I quickly excuse myself to the bathroom before Eli notices my sudden change in mood. Needing a moment to collect myself, I splash some cold water on my face, staring at my reflection in the mirror. I don't recognize the person looking back at me. I never in my life wanted to hurt anyone, let alone *murder* someone. I was so angry yesterday that I was about to do something irreversible. *This is not me.* I threatened people at the council meeting and inflicted physical pain on the twins. What I did is nothing compared to the pain they put me through over the years. Still, it's no excuse to become the same monsters that I despise. I have to figure out how to channel the anger and hurt Kevin has caused me before I lose myself completely.

Here come the waterworks. Tears fall down my cheeks. I am so sick of crying all the time. Is this my life now? Just a constant cycle of pain and tears. How do I move on from what Kevin did to me?

He looked at me like I was the only person in the world. Our dates, our conversations, our memories—it was all a lie. And to top it off, he knows who killed my father, and he's been keeping it from me. *How could he do this to me?*

"Claudette, are you ready to go?" Eli knocks on the other side of the door.

I want to stay in this bathroom and continue wallowing in my pain, but Eli is waiting for me. And I appreciate his effort in taking me to my hometown to see my best friends.

"Yeah, give me a minute," I call out, wiping away my tears with toilet paper. I apply some concealer and more eyeliner, exaggerating my angel wings to conceal any traces of my emotional breakdown.

Opening the door, I force a smile for Eli, which I'm sure he sees right through. However, he doesn't say anything. He offers me his hand and leads me to the car where Lin is waiting for us.

We arrive at Spencer's house and pull into his driveway. I jump out of the car, instantly forgetting about all of my troubles.

Spencer runs toward us, wrapping his arms around me in a tight hug. "Kevin is a jerk, and you deserve so much better," he says, meeting my gaze.

Looking away, I playfully punch him in the arm. "Thanks, Spence. Let's not discuss it; I just want to enjoy spending time with you, Nicolette, and Mitch."

"Of course, honey. Come on inside. Nicolette is waiting with snacks and games, and Mitch will stop by later."

Spencer greets Eli and Lin and leads us into the house. Nicolette meets us at the door with a slight frown on her face, walking toward me for a hug. "Hey, girl," she says, squeezing me. "We planned a game day to cheer you up."

Smiling back at her. "That sounds perfect."

"Gather around," Spencer calls out, ushering us into the den.

It's enormous and cozy, with a cabin feel to it. The wooden floors are coated with a burgundy throw rug, and a fireplace crackles straight ahead.

Eli sits next to me in a two-seater black recliner. Spencer pushes three of the single recliners in a circle around the marble table. Nicolette greets Eli and Lin, discreetly checking Lin out. *Hmm... I bet she thinks I don't notice.*

"What lie did you guys tell your parents to skip school today?" I ask, looking between Spencer and Nicolette. I'll ask her later about what she thinks of Lin.

"I told my mom I wasn't feeling well, so she might call to check on me," Nicolette says. "She's working late tonight, so it won't be a long call. And my dad has back-to-back meetings today."

Nodding, I turn to Spencer. "What about you, Spence? What did you tell your parents?"

Spencer shrugs with an over-the-top eye roll. "My father is away on business, and my mother is way too involved in my cousin's relationship drama to notice if I'm home or not." He shuffles a deck of UNO cards and adds, "Let's play UNO."

"Are we playing by the rules or house rules?" Lin, who has been quiet, pipes up.

Spencer eyes me warily. He likes to play every game by the rules.

"Let's play a round by the rules," I suggest, knowing it will make Spencer happy.

Nicolette's phone rings, and she excuses herself for a moment.

Spencer beams, dealing out the cards.

"After we play UNO, I have another game in mind that I think you'll enjoy." Nicolette winks at me when she returns, and she and Lin exchange flirty glances.

I raise an eyebrow in response.

Spencer deals out seven cards to each of us and places the rest of the deck in the center of the table. I collect my cards and group them by color.

"Who wants to go first?" Lin asks.

"Nicolette goes first. She is to the left of the dealer," Spencer says deadpan.

Eli leans in and whispers to me, "Spencer takes the rules seriously, huh?" He chuckles, and I snort.

Spencer shoots us a glare, and we quiet down.

EARTH

Nicolette flips a card over from the top of the deck. It's a green four. She goes through her cards with her nose scrunched up in concentration. Sucking her teeth, she takes a card from the deck and places down a yellow four. Lin goes next and lays down a draw-four, grinning at me.

Just my luck. I groan and draw four cards from the deck, cursing under my breath. I thought this was supposed to cheer me up, not make things worse.

"What's the color, Lin?" Eli asks, holding his cards to his chest.

"Blue."

Eli grins and puts down four cards with the same number *two* on them, leaving him with only three cards left in his hand. *Seriously?*

"Excuse me." Spencer rolls his eyes. "This is not how we play UNO."

Eli's grin grows wider, stretching from ear to ear. "Well, it's how we play." He says, pointing from Lin to himself.

Nicolette looks the other way, giggling, and Lin tries his best not to burst into laughter, his cheeks turning red.

Spencer gives me a pointed look and then leans back in his chair, muttering something under his breath as he studies his hand. He puts down a blue skip card, skipping Nicolette. It's Lin's turn again, and he puts down another draw four.

Rolling my eyes. This is ridiculous! I am not having fun. *You're being a sore loser!* Detta scolds.

"The color is red," Lin announces.

Here goes Eli again, grinning. He notices my face and seems hesitant to put down his card.

"Put a card down, dude," Spencer says impatiently.

Eli looks at us and puts down all three of his cards. "UNO out."

"What? How did you—let me see your cards?" Spencer demands as I sigh and hasten to the bathroom.

I know what you're thinking. I'm acting like a sore loser, but my life sucks right now, and I just can't handle losing at UNO on top of everything else. *I have already lost so much!*

We are supposed to be having fun, yet thoughts of Kevin keep creeping into my mind. Pushing the door shut, I sink to the floor with my back pressed against it, massaging the sides of my temple. *Ugh!* My brain feels like it's going to explode! I wish I could forget him. *How could he do this to me?*

"Claudette, open up." Nicolette knocks on the door.

"Just give me a minute." I sniffle, pulling myself off the floor.

Cracking the door open, Nicolette pushes her way in and wraps me in a tight hug. "I know you don't want to talk about it, but I'm worried about you."

I bury my face in her shoulder, tears streaming down my cheeks. "I'm a sore loser. I'm so stupid. I should have seen it coming. I can't believe I fell for his lies. I feel so betrayed and humiliated." Nicolette listens, rubbing my back and letting me cry it out. "And on top of all that, I'm an orphan!"

She forces me to look up at her. "You're not stupid, Claudette. You might be a bit of a sore loser, though," she jokes, nudging me playfully. "But you're strong and resilient. You trusted someone who didn't deserve it; that doesn't make you stupid. It just means you have a big heart. And as for being an orphan, remember that family isn't just blood. You have people who care about you, like me."

"I should have been smarter about who I trusted," I argue, wiping away my tears. "Why didn't I see it sooner?"

"Sometimes it's hard to see the truth when you're looking for the good in people." She gives me a small smile and continues. "Kevin fooled all of us. I thought he was so charming, especially when he reached out to us to meet him. I thought, *wow*, this guy is amazing for Claudette."

Clenching my fist, my breathing becomes heavy, and the bathroom lights flicker.

Nicolette grabs my hand and squeezes it. "Claudette, I need you to calm down. I know it is easier said than done, but I need you to focus on the present moment and take deep breaths."

Closing my eyes, I try to steady my racing heart. Breathing in and out slowly, again and again, I assert my control over my magic. With each breath,

I feel the tension in my body slowly dissipating.

Opening my eyes, I notice the lights have stopped flickering. *I did it!* "I think we should start referring to him as *the demon* from now on."

Nicolette laughs. "The demon it is."

There is still so much on my mind. My dad was murdered. I still haven't gotten over my mom's death, and she died years ago. The demon shattered my heart. I'm depressed. I need to find a way to heal. And to make things more complicated, I have feelings for Eli. Unable to contain the weight of my emotions any longer, I sink down the wall and find solace on the floor.

Nicolette joins me, using her index finger to lift my chin to meet her gaze. "What's on your mind?"

"It's nothing," I reply.

Nicolette's eyes search mine. "It's not just your dad's death that's bothering you. Or the demon. I know you, Detta! Talk to me."

Squinting my eyes at her. "You always see right through me."

She elbows me. "Yes! So, spill it!"

Throwing my hands up in surrender. "Fine! It's… Eli. I have feelings for him."

A smirk plays on Nicolette's lips. "I knew it! Aren't you guys fated to be together or something?"

"Yes. And that's the problem. I don't know if my feelings for him are real or just part of some prophecy." I furrow my brow in uncertainty. "Does that make sense?"

She places her hands on my shoulders and looks me straight in the eye. "Listen to me, Claudette. You and Eli had a *real* connection before you knew about magic or any prophecy. Your feelings for him are genuine, and you know it. Don't let that demon spawn fella deter you from trusting your gut. Magic or not, you and Eli have something special that goes beyond fate or prophecy from the very first day you met. This is what you told me. Was that not true?"

Nodding slowly. "Yes, it is true. Still, my heart is too broken right now, and

I don't want Eli to feel like a rebound because he is not."

"Girl, he knows he is not a rebound. He sees the real connection between you two because he told you from the get-go that you two were meant to be together," she says, narrowing her eyes. "What else is bothering you?"

"Okay, okay. We are meant to be together; I get it. I know it. It's just..." My voice trails off, and I look down at my hands.

"Claudette!" she snaps. "What is really bothering you? Don't hold back."

"Okay, fine, calm down. Sheesh! What if we start dating and then... and you know... sex comes up?"

Nicolette's brows knit together, forming a deep crease on her forehead. "I am not following."

"I lost my virginity to that demon. I'm damaged goods now," I admit, hugging my knees to my chest and pouting. "I don't want to be a h–"

"Claudette!" she cuts me off. "You can't be serious?" She lets out a soft chuckle.

My cheeks burn with embarrassment. "Yes! I am serious." I reply, rolling my eyes.

Nicolette's laughter fades, and she rolls her shoulders back. "Claudette, I didn't mean to laugh at you. I was laughing at your statement," she continues, her voice softening. "I'm going to tell you what my mother told me when she found out I lost my virginity: you may think you are in love right now, and you might be. Use this experience as a lesson, and when you find your true love, you will know it. You will feel it in your soul. He will love you and appreciate you for who you are, and he will accept you completely, flaws and all. In other words, just because you lost it to you know who, that means nothing. At the time, you were in love with him, and you felt it was right. If you and Eli decide to date and take things to the next level, then so be it. It will be because you are in love, and the timing feels right. This is not a fairy tale, and unfortunately, you didn't lose it to a prince charming and lived happily ever after. It doesn't always happen that way in real life. Still, Eli may not have been your first, but perhaps he will be your last."

My eyes widen. I'm taken aback by her words of wisdom.

She laughs, seeing my reaction. "Why are you looking at me like I have three heads?"

"When did you become so wise? We are the same age."

"Life experiences, my friend." She taps my nose playfully. "I lost my virginity before you did. And my mom had the 'birds and the bees' talk with me at a young age, sugarcoating nothing. She told me she had been with a few guys before she met my dad, but none of them compared to him. Their first time—I didn't ask to know this," she defends, her face contorting into a grimace. "Their first time was even more special because she knew that he was the one she wanted to be with forever." She rolls her eyes at the image of her parents, and I shake my head to dismiss the mental picture. "It was a beautiful story, really. Minus the visuals."

In times like this, I'm reminded of how much I miss my mom. I never got the chance to have these talks with her.

Nicolette shoots me a knowing glance, jolting me back to reality, and we both share a bittersweet smile.

"My point is that you're not damaged goods."

"You said all that to get to this as a point." I tease, nudging her.

Nicolette chuckles. "Everything I said you needed to hear."

"I did not need that image of your parents in my head," I giggle, and we burst into a fit of laughter.

"I've been living with that image since I was twelve years old. It feels good to scar you with it, too."

"Oh wow. Thanks, friend, thanks."

We continue to laugh, and I rest my head on her shoulder. "I love you."

"I love you too," she says, resting her head on mine. "You're stuck with me forever."

A comfortable silence settles between us.

"I have a question." Nicolette breaks the silence.

"Yes, Lin is single." I laugh, knowing exactly where she is going with her question.

"How did you know I was going to ask about Lin?"

"Because I know you, too."

Nicolette chuckles. "Well, you're not wrong."

We eventually stand up from the floor, still laughing and joking with each other.

"Are you going to be okay, Claudette?" She asks.

"I will be."

Nicolette gives me a reassuring smile, and we head back to the boys in the den.

Eli catches my eye from across the room when we walk in.

"Are you okay?" He mouths to me.

I smile and nod.

"Hey, Claudette!" Mitch calls out from the single recliner, waving me over.

"Aww, Mitch! I am so happy to see you!" I beam, making my way over to give him a hug.

"Let's play ten minutes in heaven," Nicolette wriggles her eyebrows.

Everyone exchanges confused glances. Then it clicks. It's supposed to be seven minutes in heaven, not ten. *This girl.*

"I am pretty sure it's seven minutes, not ten," Mitch corrects her.

"Babe, clearly she wants an extra three minutes of lip-locking." Spencer chuckles.

Nicolette winks at Spencer. "Well, who's going to be my lucky partner for those extra three minutes?"

"Lin volunteers as tribute!" I not so subtly point to Lin, who doesn't look disappointed in the slightest.

"I guess I'm the lucky one," he jokes, causing everyone to laugh along with him.

"I will set the timer for ten minutes," I announce. "Go into the other room and make it count!"

Nicolette thanks me with a wink before taking Lin's hand and leading him away.

When the timer goes off, and they don't come out, we exchange knowing glances, laughing.

"I guess they wanted to smooch a little longer, huh?" Spencer jokes, making kissing noises.

The rest of us chuckle, and we all agree that Lin and Nicolette would make a cute couple.

Mitch sits next to me, extending his arm around my shoulders. "How are you doing, Claudette?"

"I'm okay, mostly."

He squeezes my shoulder gently.

Mitch doesn't know about my magic. Spencer, Nicolette, and I agreed to leave him out of it. He knows about my father's death, and I'm sure Spencer told him about Kevin and me breaking up.

We catch up and enjoy each other's company. It feels good to be around my friends.

Nicolette and Lin finally return after twenty-something minutes, both of them looking a bit flustered.

"It's about time!" Spencer rolls his eyes teasingly.

Nicolette gives him a playful shove before tying her braids back in a bun, and Eli fist-pounds Lin. I meet Nicolette's gaze, and we share a knowing smile.

Mitch laughs and scolds Spencer to play nice, and then they share a long kiss while Nicolette and I pretend to gag, causing everyone to burst into laughter. *I needed this!*

"It's Claudette and Eli's turn," Nicolette announces when our amusement dies down.

Eli and I exchange a glance, and I bite my lip.

He extends his arm like the gentleman he is. "Shall we?"

Linking arms with him, we head to the other room.

"Ten minutes," Nicolette calls after us.

The nerve of her to shout ten minutes. Meanwhile, she and Lin were gone for twenty thousand minutes.

Eli closes the door behind us. My heart is pounding so fast, the thudding sound reverberating in my ears. We have kissed before, but this is different. This kiss will mean something more to us. I am single. He is single. We are attracted to one another, not to mention the fated lover's thing.

"We don't have to do this if you don't want to," Eli says, breaking the silence between us.

I want to kiss him. I want Eli to heal my broken heart and make me forget I was ever with that demon. But he would be a rebound. I can't do this! I don't want to do this to him.

I'm ready to bolt out of the room, but before I can make a move, Eli gently takes my hand and looks into my eyes. "Claudette, what are you thinking?"

Taking a deep breath, I feel the weight of my emotions pressing down on me. "I'm just scared, Eli. Scared of hurting you," I admit. "I'm broken. I don't deserve you. You don't deserve to be a rebound! You deserve better."

Eli digests my words before responding, "Claudette, you're not broken. You're scared, and that's okay. We can take things slow until you're ready, no matter how long it takes."

My breath catches in my throat, and a wave of anticipation washes over me, making my stomach churn.

"I wouldn't be a rebound, Claudette. I would finally be yours, as you have been mine since the day electricity flowed throughout our bodies."

His words wrap around me like a warm blanket. He feels like home, like safety.

"I will wait for you until you are ready to be loved by a real man. Because that's what you deserve." He grasps my waist, pulling me closer to him in one quick motion. I gasp at his sudden proximity, feeling his heartbeat against my chest. He kisses me slowly, his lips soft and gentle against mine, before picking up the pace and knocking the air out of my lungs. This kiss is different from the others we've shared. He has been holding back. As electric shocks ricochet between our bodies, blue, brown, and gold lights circle around us. My back presses against the door as our kiss deepens, and I feel his length pressing against me. I can tell he is trying hard to control himself, which causes butterflies to flutter in my stomach.

When our lips part, he brushes his thumb over my cheek. "Baby, you're worth waiting for, and I will mend your heart with every beat of mine until it is no longer broken."

Chapter 10

The Dark Plan

Kevin's point of view:

It has been two weeks since that little slut tried to murder me. *Unbelievable!* I wasted all those weeks pretending to be interested in her just so she could try to kill me. *Once I regain my magic, I will make sure she never sees the light of day again!* I am glad her father is dead because he won't be able to protect her from what's coming next. Too bad I wasn't the one to end his life. However, I believe in the saying that revenge is best served cold, and I am determined to make her pay for what she did to me.

I anticipated that Claudette would use the truth potion on me, so I kept my involvement in her father's murder to a minimum. Still, the satisfaction of watching the fear in his eyes as he grasped his fate was sealed was sweeter than anything I could have imagined. A slight smirk tugs at the corners of my lips as I remember the look in his eyes. Rubbing my hands together, I realize that my plan is succeeding. Claudette's reunion with her father in the afterlife is imminent.

Glancing at my watch, I notice the time. Malcolm should be on his way over with the Earth necklace and ring that Claudette's father was wearing on the day of his death. He has been holding onto it for safekeeping until this very moment. Tonight, when the Sun, Moon, and Earth align, I will call upon Antus, the leader of the Shadow World. I have devoted myself to him in exchange for my magic, and tonight is the night it will rightfully return to me.

In my dreams, Antus revealed a startling revelation about the town. There is a covert presence of Earth witches posing as Sun or Moon witches. The necklace will reveal the truth, and the ring will guide me to the Earth's spell book, a tome known for its formidable magic.

All of my pursuits have been dedicated to Antus's name to restore my magic. In an attempt to prevent my malevolence, my parents—both Sun witches—believed that removing my magic would be effective in saving me from the darkness. They couldn't have been more wrong. They thought removing my magic would stop the dreams from Antus, but it didn't. I enjoy killing people—especially those who aren't supposed to occupy this realm. There is nothing wrong with me, and if my parents had never revoked my magic, I wouldn't have suffered the torment of being powerless. For far too long, I have concealed my true self, feigning to care and be kind like the other witches in this town. Pretending to be someone I am not has been draining me. Finally, I will regain my magic and embrace the essence of who I truly am! *My parents should be proud!*

All children born into the same coven are bound to Antus, and it is time for us to grow in numbers. We will force Sun and Moon witches to breed with their own kind to create an army of children born to serve Antus as king. We will completely obliterate the remaining Earth witches and anyone who opposes us, once and for all.

Antus has visited me in my dreams for years with instructions to reclaim my power. Every dream is akin to a blazing furnace, consuming me from the inside out. Still, the pain of the dreams is nothing compared to the power I will wield once I complete his bidding. Antus instructed me to slaughter seventeen Earth witches in his honor, and I have carried out his orders without hesitation. Earth witches are targeted because their magic surpasses all the other witches, making them formidable opponents. My mother has assisted me in killing sixteen of them. Although Chance never accepted his magic, he was born an Earth witch, and that served as a sacrifice in Antus's name. His death was also necessary to obtain his Earth necklace and ring, and the only way to acquire them was through his demise. Now, I have one more witch to kill before I can restore my magic and defeat Claudette with Antus by my side!

Three weeks prior to Claudette and her family's arrival in Mashalville, Tanya and I concocted a scheme for me to cozy up to Claudette to gain her trust. I initially hoped for a platonic friendship with her. However, her subtle flirtations made it clear that she would be more receptive to a romantic relationship. In one of my dreams, Antus disclosed that I wouldn't be able to kill Claudette without my magic. I needed to use her attraction to me to my advantage and keep her away from her fated lover because once they admit their love to one another and perform a spell, they would be a powerful force to be reckoned with. This required me to walk a fine line between gaining her trust and keeping her at arm's length.

Pretending to reciprocate her feelings was insufferable. It felt like I was walking through a maze of thorny roses, the vibrant red petals masking the prickly reality of our lives. The sound of her voice was like nails on a chalkboard grating against my eardrums. The scent of her perfume was suffocating with its sickly sweetness that clung to my skin long after she had left the room. Each interaction with her brought a sense of dread and discomfort. Tanya had to coach me the entire time I was with her. Sex was the worst part. I found solace by visualizing Tanya in Claudette's place; she was the only one who could genuinely arouse me. Every time we had sex, my mind would drift to thoughts of Tanya, her touch, her scent, and her voice. It allowed me to perform with Claudette, albeit reluctantly. Tanya is my true mate. She would send me naughty texts right before I saw Claudette, which helped me get through those revolting moments. *Thank you, Antus!* I am finally free from the burden of Claudette Richardson's presence.

Knock, knock.

I open the door, expecting to see Malcolm standing there, but instead, I am met with Tanya's radiant beauty.

My lips curl into a delightful smirk at the sight of her. She is wearing a short skirt and a low-cut top that highlights her ample breasts perfectly.

"Where is Tristan?"

"He will be here soon." Tanya steps inside, closing the door behind her. "We have about thirty minutes." She says suggestively, stripping down to her lacy lingerie.

Licking my lips, I observe her body intently. She is a sensual sight to behold, and being inside her is a welcome distraction. Tristan does not know about Tanya and me, and I like to keep it that way. So, we have to be quick.

"Come here," I growl, gripping her by the neck and closing the distance between us with a hungry kiss.

Her scent is intoxicating, and I lose myself at the moment as we quickly make our way to the sofa. Clothes are discarded in a frenzy, and she straddles my lap, her body moving in sync with mine.

Twenty minutes later, our pleasurable escapade concludes, and we quickly dress before Tristan arrives.

I grab my phone to call Malcolm and make sure he's still on schedule. He is currently with Libby, but he assures me he will be here in ten minutes. Libby has been keeping up pretenses with Claudette; she does not know that Libby was the one who killed her father.

"Malcolm will be here soon," I say to Tanya as we finish getting dressed.

Tanya nods, adjusting her hair. "Where are we with the plan?"

Gripping her neck once more, I press my lips against hers, bruising her skin. "Everything is going according to plan," I whisper, a sinister smile playing on my lips. "I just need to locate the imposters in this town before finally regaining my power."

"Excellent!" she replies, a wide grin spreading across her face.

Casting a wink at her, I turn and head to my room to fetch the Shadow

EARTH

World book from my drawer. The book is black, with Antus's name engraved on the front and coated with his dry blood. I grab my dagger and walk over to the snake cage in the corner of my room. It hisses, but I quickly silence it with a swift strike to its head with the dagger and discard its body in a bag.

I meet Tanya in the living room, and she welcomes Tristan at the door with a kiss. Tristan acknowledges me with a nod before following Tanya inside.

When Malcolm arrives, it's showtime. Tanya hands me a dark brown bowl with the snake head, three ounces of burdock root, and one pound of dead grass. I throw the Earth necklace into the bowl and light the contents with a match. Flipping through the ancient book of Antus, my eyes quickly scan the pages in search of the precise spell that I must recite. The spell is in the language of Antuson.

"Ah nu ja ka. Si ra ka. Ah, nu fig tu. Sap kai ru." I chant four times.

The lights flicker erratically, and a cloud of black smoke billows out of the bowl. Antus has granted me his blessing.

The black smoke swirls around my phone, and its purpose is to find Earth witches hiding in plain sight. I open the GPS app on my phone and watch as the map pinpoints five separate locations of the hidden witches.

"This looks like Jimmy's house," Tanya says, pointing to one of the locations.

"Some are our teachers' homes," Tristan adds, looking at the other pins on the map.

Mr. Goatfair and Mr. Max are Earth witches. Lin, *Eli's best friend,* is also on the list. *Two Earth warlocks living under the same roof!* The fourth location is Jimmy's house, and the fifth location is *Claudette.*

These parasites have been living right under our noses this whole time, completely unnoticed. I will derive immense pleasure from ending all of their pathetic lives. However, right now, I only need one of them to sacrifice to tap into my power.

"Who will it be?" Tanya muses.

Jessie Max and Adam Goatfair have been practicing magic for years.

Successfully concealing their status as Earth warlocks for such a prolonged duration is beyond my comprehension.

"Either Lin or Jimmy," I reply, my mind racing with delight.

"You have to make the final call, Kevin," Tanya says, her voice filled with uncertainty.

They look at me expectantly, awaiting my decision.

As much as I want to execute Lin to see the look on Eli's face, it makes more sense to kill Jimmy. He wouldn't see it coming.

"Jimmy," I decide.

The group nods in agreement.

"I will call him to meet us here," Tanya says, walking away to dial his number.

"My work here is done," Malcolm states, packing up his things. "I will take the ring back to Libby's and update her on what's happening."

"Good idea," I nod. "We don't want the ring and necklace to sit in the same place for too long."

Malcolm looks at me with a knowing expression and leaves my apartment.

Tanya returns, saying that Jimmy will be arriving in twenty minutes.

"What did you tell him?"

Tanya shrugs. "I just told him we were having game night."

Twenty minutes later...

"Jimmy is here!" Tanya shouts from the living room.

Rummaging through my dresser, I search for the Ne-aik-eart dagger Tanya procured for me. Changing into a long-sleeved black shirt, I slip the dagger up my sleeve. Before leaving my room, I gather a rat's tail and spider legs from my collection of ingredients for the spell.

"Hey Jimmy, ready for game night?" I ask casually, walking into the living room.

"Uh, yeah." He scratches the back of his neck, his eyes flitting between the three of us. "I am surprised you invited me."

I give him a reassuring smile, reaching for an apple cider. The sound of the can opening fills the air. I offer him a drink in an effort to put him at ease. "Of course, we're all friends here."

Tristan stifles a chuckle, and Tanya nudges him with her elbow.

Jimmy's shoulders relax, and a smile forms on his face as he accepts the drink. "Thanks," he says, taking a sip.

After a few minutes of small talk, his defenses begin to lower, permitting me to make the swift and fatal move of slitting his neck with the dagger.

Jimmy's body slumps to the ground, and his eyes open in shock as his magic drains away. Tanya throws me a kitchen knife, and I relentlessly stab the blade into his chest, snuffing out his life while Tristan and Tanya rejoice in the success of our plan.

With a calm demeanor, I meticulously clean the blade and then turn towards them, a sinister smile forming on my face as I utter, "It's finally come to fruition. I will have my magic back!"

Tristan and Tanya exchange a knowing look, their excitement palpable.

Adding the rat tail and spider legs to the bowl with the other ingredients, I thumb through the pages to find the spell that will restore my magic. The final component required is the vital life force coursing through Jimmy's veins.

With a wave of his hand, Tristan harnesses his magic to draw Jimmy's blood into the bowl.

"Ready?" Tanya asks gleefully.

Nodding, I begin to chant the incantation two times. "In this witch's hour, I call upon my master's power. Give me back what my heart desires. Give me back my divine power."

As the incantation ends, an eerie ambiance fills the room, causing the air to grow cold. A surge of energy courses through me and sets my skin ablaze, emanating a searing heat from deep within. I bite back on my screams. A thick, black liquid swivels around my forearms, trickling down my fingertips. The lights flicker, and electric crackling fills the room. It's as if gravity has disappeared, and I feel weightless. Hovering in mid-air, I feel a surge of electricity as bolts of lightning dance across my skin. The pain is excruciating, but I push through, each breath feeling like fire in my lungs. My magic is finding its way back to me.

After what feels like an eternity, my body descends slowly back to the floor, the black liquid dissipating into my skin. I stand tall, feeling my awakened power coursing through my veins, marking the completion of the spell.

My magic has returned.

Chapter 11

Family Reunion

As the morning sun rises, its radiant rays pass through the fabric of my brown curtains, casting a spellbinding glow that fills the entire room. Eli's words live rent-free in my mind: *"Baby, you're worth waiting for, and I will mend your heart with every beat of mine until it is no longer broken."* The mere thought of it makes my heart race with excitement. Rolling over on my back, I stare at the ceiling. I want to be with Eli. However, the events involving that demon have left me feeling torn and uncertain. Can I trust Eli? Should I even be thinking about another relationship? Or should I focus on who killed my father? *Who murdered your father?* My inner voice shouts. When considering the available alternatives, it becomes evident that the last option is the most logical and rational choice.

Rolling my eyes at Detta's nagging voice in my head, I know she is right. Finding my father's killer is my top priority before anything else. That doesn't stop my mind from wandering back to Eli and the feelings he stirs within me. Will he break my heart like Kevin did?

Finding out about Kevin's betrayal broke me. I can't let myself be hurt like that again. My heart is still healing from the devastating loss of my mother and the tragic murder of my father. Their deaths shattered me into countless pieces, each shard serving as a painful reminder of their absence. And Kevin only added to that pain. On top of the relentless bullying and torment I endured from the demon twins and at school, I need to protect myself from any more heartbreak. The emotional scars are still fresh and raw. *Why was I put on this Earth to suffer so much pain and heartache? What is my purpose? Why am I here? I mean, seriously, why do I even exist?*

Tears start to well up in my eyes and then cascade down my cheeks. "God, if you're listening, please tell me your plan for me. Show me a sign—anything to let me know that there's a reason for all this suffering."

No response.

"Jaju or… Antus, why gift me with magic?"

No response.

Each question I hurl into the air is met with silence, leaving the empty sound of my own voice. Being alone in this world with no clear purpose or direction terrifies me to the core, and thoughts of ending my own life creep in. The future appears bleak and offers little to no hope for a brighter tomorrow. The little voice in my head calls me a hypocrite. Remembering my conversation with Isabel, I told her, *"I wanted to end my life. I wanted the pain I felt to be over. But trust me when I say someone needs you."*

Who needs me now?

No one.

More tears stream down my face.

I have no family left in my life.

A gentle knock on my door interrupts the chaos swirling inside me.

"Claudette, are you awake?" Eli calls out.

To be completely honest, I would rather not be awake right now. My pain is something I desperately long to be rid of.

When I don't respond, he walks right in. I quickly hide under the covers to hide my half-naked body. *What happened to not barging in?*

"You are awake. Why didn't you answer me?"

I let out an exaggerated sigh.

"Claudette, come out from under the covers," Eli pleads, sitting down on the edge of the bed.

I peek out from under the covers, my eyes red and swollen. I am not in the mood to face anyone.

"I just need some time alone right now," I murmur, avoiding his gaze. "I am completely broken, and I don't want to talk about it." Wiping the tears from my eyes, I turn away from him and curl up into a ball.

"I understand, Claudette," he says softly. "I'll be here when you're ready to talk, but just know that I *need* you. Please don't do anything that would cause you to leave me."

My breath catches in my throat, and I hold myself tighter. *How did he know what I was thinking?* He sees inside my soul.

When I don't respond, Eli gets up to leave, closing the door behind him. I stay curled up on the bed, closing my eyes to block out the world and drift off to dreamland.

A few hours later, I still don't feel any better. I do as Ms. Hudson suggested, grabbing my diary from my nightstand to write it all down.

Dear Diary,

Me again. To be honest, my current mental state is not very good. With each passing moment, I feel myself descending further into the dark, suffocating depths of the void. I thought I was past this. While I had convinced myself that I had successfully moved past this feeling of not wanting to be alive, the overwhelming grief and longing for my father have brought it back to the forefront of my mind. Why did he have to be murdered? I still don't understand God's plan for me. What is my purpose? I feel alone and broken. I loved Kevin. I still love him… How could I still love someone who used me? I hate myself for allowing him to deceive me. When I first met Eli, I knew we had an undeniable connection, but I was a fool. Instead of listening to Eli, I stayed with that demon. Eli is too good for me. Being happy is not something I deserve, and neither is being alive.

Closing my diary, I toss it to the side, closing my eyes once again.

Five days later...

Eli barges into my room and opens up the curtains, letting the sunlight flood in. I squint my eyes at the brightness, pulling the covers over my head to shield myself from the light.

"I can't stand to see you like this, Claudette! I am not letting you wallow in self-pity anymore," he says. "I called Ms. Hudson, and you have an emergency session with her today. Take a shower, get dressed, and eat. Now!"

I groan in protest. Who does Eli think he is, ordering me around like this? Still, deep down, I know he's right.

"Claudette!" he calls out, his voice stern.

Annoyance bubbles up inside me, and I roll my eyes, hauling myself out of bed.

Eli stands in the doorway, arms crossed, with a pointed look on his face. He knows me too well.

Dragging my feet and grumbling under my breath, I reluctantly head towards the bathroom to shower and get dressed.

I go through my morning routine, meeting Eli in the kitchen, where he has breakfast waiting for me.

A heavy silence hangs between us, a clear indication of his disappointment and anger. Sighing loudly, I lean on the kitchen counter. He prepared a simple breakfast of toast and eggs.

Eli snatches the butter off the counter and shoves it into the fridge, his jaw clenched tight.

I take a bite of toast, and his eyes bore into me.

He finally breaks the silence, his voice cold and clipped. "You are having a session with Gabriella and the twins today."

Spitting out a piece of toast. "I'm sorry. Repeat that back to me. I must have misheard you." I twist my index finger in my ear to clear out some wax because I want to make sure I heard him correctly.

Eli's eyes narrow. "You heard me right," he says deadpan.

Woah! What is with him today? He is usually so sweet to me, not this cold.

"What is your problem, Eli?"

His jaw clenches as he shouts, "*You* are my problem, Claudette!"

A knot tightens in my stomach, and I lower my gaze. I feel awful knowing that I'm the cause.

"Trust me, I get it. You experienced a lot of traumas. You lost both of your parents, and Kevin broke your heart. I know you're hurting, but life goes on, Claudette!" I flinch at his words, and he lifts my chin up gently, his eyes softening. "I love you, and I'm here for you. However, you have to let me in. Nicolette, Spencer, Mitch, Lin, Destiny, and Isabel all love you too. Don't shut us out. We all dealt with our own traumas, but we keep pushing forward. That's what you need to do. Push through the pain, Claudette. I know it doesn't seem like it now, but you are strong enough to overcome this." He holds my hand tight, his touch grounding me in reality. "My parents are evil people. They have never shown me any love." His voice trembles with pain as he continues, a rawness that cuts through the air. "My father has always been absent and never stepped up to protect my brother and me from our mother. My mother ran the show and called all the shots. She was emotionally abusive and manipulative, constantly tearing us down with her words. She belittled me, told me I was useless, and wished she never had me. Do you know what that does to a four-year-old? I wanted to be loved by my mom. And I wasn't. I was four, wishing I had never been born. I remember feeling so small and helpless, and there were plenty of times I contemplated taking my life. The difference is my parents wouldn't have cared. Do you think your mother and father would agree with you taking your own life?"

I shake my head, tears well up in my eyes. *How does he know I want to die?*

"Claudette, you were put on this Earth for a reason, and it's time you start believing in yourself. God makes no mistakes!"

As I wipe away my tears, I lift my gaze towards him, speechless and unsure of what to say.

"I'm sorry, Eli." I choke out.

I need to get through this. *I will!*

He sighs. "Are you ready to go?"

Not really.

"Why am I having a session with Gabriella and the twins?"

"You were locked in your room for a week, not responding to calls or texts. Gabriella reached out to me. She seemed worried about you, so she suggested a session with her and the twins to make things right," Eli explains.

My eyes widen in surprise, and I nervously scratch the back of my neck. "I guess I'm ready."

This is my first therapy session in over a week. When I get out of Eli's car, I see Ms. Hudson with Mr. Handsome—the same man she was with on the day my father was murdered. Things seem to be getting serious between them. *Good for Ms. Hudson.*

"I'll see you later, Libby," he says to her, nodding in my direction as he walks past me.

A rosy hue spreads across Ms. Hudson's cheeks. *Libby?*

"I'll be here when your session is done," Eli calls out, and I give him a small smile.

"Hi, Claudette. How are you feeling today?" Ms. Hudson asks with a warm smile, inviting me inside.

"Okay, I suppose."

She leads me to her office, where I settle into the familiar chair. "We will give Gabriella, Marissa, and Crissy a few more minutes to arrive before we begin."

I shift uncomfortably in my seat. One therapy session won't undo the years of emotional and physical abuse they have caused.

Ms. Hudson notes my reaction in her notebook before looking up at me with a sympathetic expression. "Gabriella suggested we all meet as a family. This is a good place to start."

Scoffing internally, I resist the urge to roll my eyes. "Ms. Hudson, I don't mean to be disrespectful, but those people are not my family. My *real* family is dead."

She winces at the last part of my sentence, scribbling in her notepad. *I wonder what she writes in there.*

Gabriella, Marissa, and Crissy stroll into the room right when Ms. Hudson finishes jotting down her notes. *Oh great!*

"Excellent!" Ms. Hudson exclaims, clapping her hands together. "Now that everyone is here, we can begin. Please take a seat."

Gabriella sits down, and the demon twins reluctantly follow suit. Snickering to myself, I wonder how long this family session will last before the chaos begins.

"Why do we need to be here?" Marissa grits out, clearly not thrilled about being here either.

Gabriella tucks Marissa's hair behind her ear. "Because, sweetheart, we are a family."

Sucking my teeth. "We are not a family!" I sneer, crossing my arms defiantly.

"I agree," Crissy adds through gritted teeth. "Blacky is not our family!"

"Oh, wow!" My voice drips with sarcasm. "You can speak for yourself now, huh?"

Crissy shoots me a glare. "I hate you!"

"The feeling is mutual!" I retort, glaring back at her.

Crissy whispers something incoherent under her breath, which causes me to float into the air.

"Put me down!" I yell, "Right now, Crissy!"

Crissy smirks, and with a sudden jolt, I plummet to the floor, my knee colliding with it. The impact sends a sharp pain shooting up my leg.

"Now we're even," her smirk widens.

Oh, so we're using magic now?

I struggle to stand up, ignoring the pain in my knee. "Fine, let's play dirty." I summon my own spell to retaliate against Crissy, preparing to shatter every bone in her body when Gabriella suddenly intervenes.

"Enough!" she asserts, her voice cutting through the room. "We are a family."

My blood boils. She needs to stop saying that. We are *not* a family. When has she ever treated me like her own? How many times has she covered for her daughters when they bullied me? I clench my fists, my anger pulsing through me. *I've had enough!*

"We are *not* a family!" I growl, glaring at Gabriella. "You have never treated me as such, and now you want to act like you care? It's too late for that!" I limp out of the office as quickly as possible, leaving Gabriella stunned in my wake.

Chapter 12

Attack

Eli is waiting for me outside when I storm out of the office, and he knows not to say anything as I fume in silence. He starts the engine, and we head back to the apartment. Once we're home, I rush to the bathroom and slam the door shut, needing to be alone to cool off. Running the water as hot as I can stand, I try to declutter my thoughts under the soothing cascade of steam. Water brings me a sense of solace.

All these years, Gabriella has been an awful stepmother to me. She may have loved my dad, but she never showed me an ounce of kindness. She knew how her daughters treated me, yet she did nothing to stop it. There was always some lame excuse for their behavior. Now, she wants to play nice and pretend like everything is okay by saying *"We are a family."* Such nonsense. I am over her, and I am over the whole situation. My father is dead, and he was the last tie to those people. They will never be my family.

Stepping out of the shower, I wrap myself in a towel heading to my room to get dressed. I pass the living room, where Eli, Isabel, Lin, and Destiny are standing with worried expressions on their faces. *What's going on?* Hurrying to my room, I throw on a red T-shirt and gray sweatpants before returning to the living room to see what's happening.

Lin is pacing the room with his hands clasped behind his back when I walk in, and the others are waiting anxiously for him to speak.

"Lin, what's going on?" I ask.

He stops pacing and turns to face us, his expression grave. Sighing heavily, he says, "I have to tell you guys something important."

What is he about to say? Everyone's eyes are fixed on him, waiting for him to continue. If he says he had something to do with my father's death, I will lose it!

"I am an Earth witch." He pauses, letting the words sink in.

Destiny, Isabel, and I exchange confused glances while Eli remains neutral. *Does he already know?*

"What do you mean?" Destiny asks, breaking the silence.

Lin takes a deep breath before explaining the truth about his powers and how he has been hiding them from us all this time. "Kevin and his minions killed Jimmy. I received confirmation from Adam." Lin reveals.

The girls gasp while Eli clenches his jaw.

"You mean Adam, as in our teacher? Mr. Goatfair?" I furrow my brows.

Lin nods. "The battle has begun. Kevin needed to kill one more Earth witch to regain his powers. Jimmy was an Earth witch as well, hiding in plain sight. Kevin completed his final sacrifice, and now his powers are fully restored. He will be coming for all of us." Lin faces me with a rigid gaze. "Especially you, Claudette, and if he kills you, he will be invincible."

A cold shiver runs down my spine, and I have to sit down to steady myself. I bury my forehead in my hands, trying to process the gravity of Lin's words. *Kevin has his magic back.* Eli sits beside me, gently positioning my head to rest on his chest. I hear the rhythmic thumping of his heartbeat against my ear.

"Our History of Magic teacher, Mr. Goatfair, is actually an Earth witch—*warlock*?" Destiny asks, her eyes widened in realization. "How many Earth witches are there in town?"

"Yes," Lin confirms. "And there's only four of us left. Myself, Adam, Mr. Max, and Claudette." Destiny's and Isabel's eyes widen even further.

"I am sorry for deceiving you all for so long, but it was necessary for my protection," Lin apologizes. "Earth witches and warlocks are targets. My father was killed because he was one, and my mother died while trying to protect him. Mr. Goatfair took me in after their deaths. He knew of my lineage, and I don't know where I would be if he hadn't adopted me." Lin pauses, a somber expression crossing his face. "Adam sought help from Ms. Caron to create a potion to mask my true identity from the Witch Council under the assumption I took after my mother's coven."

"Ms. Caron knows you are an Earth witch?" Isabel asks in disbelief.

"Yes," Lin confirms matter-of-factly.

Eli clears his throat, and all eyes turn to him. "My parents told Jeremiah that Kevin's parents took his magic away before he turned seventeen in hopes that Antus would stop visiting him. His parents were removed from the council shortly after. Despite my parents being evil, they wanted no dealings with the likes of Antus. Jeremiah recently alerted me that Kevin's mother assisted in killing Earth witches against her will."

Lin's eyebrows snap together, creating a crease between them, and his eyes grow wide. "You mean to tell me Kevin's mother had something to do with the death of my parents?"

"And mine?" Isabel asks.

"My mother?" Destiny adds.

Eli nods. "She could have, but I'm not sure. We will get to the bottom of this."

"Don't you and Jeremiah hate each other?" Isabel asks, narrowing her eyes at Eli.

Eli shakes his head. "It's an act to throw off suspicion from our parents."

"What about the prophecy?" I say, and my friends turn to me. "Kevin said we are fated to be together."

Destiny scoffs, Isabel rolls her eyes, Lin raises an eyebrow, and Eli sighs.

"The prophecy states that there is one Earth witch fated to be with a Moon witch, born in the same month, and she would be the most powerful

Earth witch the world has known. Together, the couple would be unmatched," Eli explains, fixing his gaze on me.

The room falls silent, and everyone looks between Eli and me. Butterflies flutter in my stomach, and I try to push them away by directing my attention to Lin. "How were you, Mr. Goatfair, and Mr. Max able to stop me that day at school?"

Lin's lips curve into a knowing smirk. "Ah, that was all thanks to the talisman, Ny-rob-son."

"A what?"

"There is no question that you are the most powerful witch to walk the Earth. We used the talisman to combine our magic to stop you from murdering Kevin and his clan. We were only able to use it because you haven't reached your full potential yet. We couldn't let you kill them, even if they deserved it. It would have taken you out as well," he elaborates.

Rolling my eyes, I scoff at his explanation. "Thank you for the mini history lesson." I get up and walk to my room, feeling the weight of his words sink in.

Pacing my room back and forth, annoyance settles in my chest. *Why does the fate of the world fall on me?* I am supposedly the most powerful being to walk this Earth, except I feel far from it. With Kevin now in possession of his magic, I feel powerless against him. I nearly lost myself when I tried to kill him and his minions, and he had no magic then. *"It would have taken you out."* Lin's words echo in my mind. What did he mean by that? *The magic was draining you.* My inner voice whispers.

There's a knock on my door. "Babe, can I come in?" Eli's voice breaks through my thoughts.

When I don't reply, he just waltzes right in. *It seems like neither of us has an issue with intruding on each other.*

"I can't do this right now, Eli," I tell him, my voice shaky. "I'm sorry I gave Lin an attitude. I am not upset with him. I am just overwhelmed by everything that's happening."

"I understand, Claudette. Still, we need to devise a plan. Kevin has his magic, and there is no telling when he will come after you." He tries to reason with me, but I can't focus on planning right now.

I let out a soft sigh, my eyes reflecting a mix of emotions. I know he's right—it is all just too much for one person.

"Eli, I still love him," I confess, my voice barely above a whisper and my eyes lowering to avoid his gaze. I am embarrassed to face his reaction. However, it's unrealistic to expect that I can simply erase my feelings within a matter of weeks. "I am heartbroken, depressed, and grieving all at once. How can I go up against him? I barely made it out the last time. My magic was draining me."

The mattress dips as he sits down beside me, running his fingers through his hair with a soft rustling sound. "Give me your hands."

Furrowing my brows, I meet his gaze.

"Do you trust me?"

Nodding slowly, I place my hands in his, unsure of where he's going with this.

He holds them tight, closing his eyes to recite a spell. "I call upon the Moon and Earth to combine our powers. Give us access and sight, and make us one with the Moon, Earth, and night."

The spell takes effect. Blue, brown, and gold lights swirl around us, filling the air with a mystical glow and merging our magic into an enchanting force. His magic courses through me, emanating from my chest and filling me with powerful energy. The sensation is a paradoxical combination of pleasure and discomfort, leaving a prickling sensation that's challenging to put into words. It taps into my inner strength, and a sudden surge electrifies my body, sending a vibrant jolt racing through my veins. I can almost see the crackling energy as it flows, like an intense lightning storm swaying beneath my skin. The tingling sensation intensifies, radiating from my core and spreading outward, reaching its peak at my fingertips. It's as if tiny sparks of power are eager to burst forth, illuminating the surrounding air.

The energy flows into Eli, and an exhilarating transformation unfolds before my eyes. His once ordinary eyes undergo a profound change, shifting into a captivating blend of dark brown and shimmering gold. With a sudden burst of power, he floats into the air, his hands slipping from mine. My magic is engulfing him as if it's devouring his very essence. As he descends to the floor, I feel an electric shock in my eyes, too.

My previous sense of power has transformed into an overwhelming feeling of invincibility. In a moment of complete certainty and without any hesitation, I find myself instinctively embracing Eli, desperate for the solace and reassurance that his familiar touch brings.

"What did you do to us?"

Eli smiles, a hint of allure and confidence radiating from his face. "I was only able to tap into merging our magic because you *love* me."

"W–what?" Chuckling nervously, my eyes dart from his face to the floor.

Eli tilts my chin up, locking eyes with me, and a sexy smile traces along his defined lips. "We are fated to be together, and you accepted that. Earth witches can access magic at any time of the day. And I am the strongest at night. Kevin is smart. He will most likely launch his attack against us during the day when I am at my weakest. But you finally admitted to yourself that you love me. *You. Love. Me.*" Eli's grin grows wider. "Our souls are intertwined, uniting our magic and granting us the strength we need to face him. Our powers wouldn't have merged if you didn't love me. And now, we are unstoppable together."

Before I can even respond, a commotion outside interrupts our conversation. The noise resonates through the air, resembling the deafening blasts of exploding bombs.

Eli and I sprint to the living room to see what is happening outside through the window. Kevin's minions wreak havoc in the streets, causing chaos and destruction wherever they go. My heart races with fear and adrenaline. My breath quickens. And a wave of panic washes over me as I start hyperventilating. The sound of my own rapid, shallow breaths fills the air, drowning out any other noise. My chest tightens. The weight of helplessness engulfs me as my knees tremble and my palms dampen with sweat. I struggle to maintain my composure. There is no way I will win, especially now that Kevin has his magic. With each rushing thought, a wave of dizziness consumes me, and the room slowly fades to black.

Resting against the wall to steady my breathing, Isabel sprints to my side. Lin, Destiny, and Eli rush outside to face the demon.

They don't stand a chance against him.

"This is ridiculous!" Isabel yells, rolling her eyes as she pulls me up. "Are you okay, mama?"

My eyes swell up with tears. "I don't think I can go up against him. My magic nearly drained me that day in school."

Isabel shakes her head. "That's because you were trying to take all of them out. You need to focus on one at a time. I need you to get yourself together. You can do this, mama!"

She is right. War is happening—the great fight between good and evil. I look out the window again, trying to build confidence. Kevin hovers mid-air, bathed in a swirling crimson mist. Sinister horns protrude from his head, and his eyes glow with a malevolent light, devoid of any trace of humanity. At the sight of him now, the little ounce of love I had left for him vanishes entirely. He is a demon.

"Where is she?!" Kevin bellows.

He is after me. This is payback for trying to kill him.

I start to pant heavily. "I can't do this. I don't think I can do it. I can't–"

Isabel smacks me on the arm, snapping me out of my panic. *"¡Tú puedes hacerlo!"*

Huh? My Spanish is a little rusty.

"You can do it, Claudette! *¡Tú puedes hacerlo!*" She repeats, "We must fight back!"

Isabel is right. We must fight back!

Moving towards the door, I exhale a sharp breath, preparing myself for the confrontation ahead.

Chaos surrounds me. People are running in all directions, screaming. Isabel joins Destiny to fight against the twins. Of course, the twins would side with Kevin. They have a deep-rooted hatred for me.

My eyes shift to Lin, who is taking on Tristan and Tanya by himself. Eli and Kevin are facing off, their faces contorted with rage as they clash. Eli hurls vibrant blue and pure white, shimmering gold fireballs at Kevin, crackling with energy as they explode on impact. Kevin retaliates with fiery red orbs, with searing heat waves emanating from each one. They soar through the air, leaving trails of smoke and scorch marks in their wake, attacking one another in a continuous loop.

Suddenly, Tanya breaks away from her fight with Lin, sprinting towards me with determination in her eyes. Using her extraordinary abilities, she effortlessly propels me into the air and back down, causing a resounding crash as I collide with the ground. My left wrist snaps upon contact with the hard pavement. I scream in agony, distracting Eli, and Kevin flings him into a tree. My eyes widen in horror as he crumples to the ground and his elbow bone protrudes from his skin.

"Nooo!" I screech, and Kevin grins sadistically when he sees me. He sends Tanya a knowing look, and she nods at his silent command.

Summoning all my strength to push through the pain, I stand up to get to Eli, who is currently incapacitated. Still, Tanya is blocking my path by conjuring flaming purple spheres and throwing them in my direction. The first strike sends a searing pain through my arm as the flames scorch my skin, leaving behind blistering burns. I grit my teeth and keep moving forward, determined to reach Eli. Tanya is on the brink of launching another fireball in my direction when a protective force field materializes around me, deflecting the attack and giving me a moment to assess the situation. My eyes dart around, trying to identify the individual—*individuals* behind the barrier, as I am determined to thank them. It's Ms. Billie, Ms. Caron, Mr. Goatfair, and Mr. Max.

They are shouting in unison and channeling their energy to help me. Mr. Goatfair and Ms. Caron combine their strengths to create a powerful counterattack, sending Tanya stumbling back.

"Get to Eli!" Mr. Goatfair shouts.

Sprinting towards Eli as fast as I can, I dodge the enemy along the way. He is unconscious but breathing. Struggling to lift his dead weight off the ground, I manage to hoist him up when a fireball comes hurtling towards us and explodes in a burst of flames, knocking us off balance. My good wrist breaks my fall as I shield Eli from the impact. Tristan hovers above us, bathed in a magnetic glow of red and orange lights. My pulse quickens, each beat resonating with the growing anger that boils inside me. All rationality is replaced by an unyielding and burning determination. *I've had enough!* While I may not be able to defeat Kevin at the moment, Tristan is no match for me.

Heal. Healing my wrists, I levitate, soaring above my enemy. Channeling all of my energy to Tristan and utilizing the incredible amplification provided by Eli, I trigger a rupture in the vein inside his brain, resulting in his swift and irreversible death. It is eerily quiet as his limp body crashes against the cement, fracturing his skull on impact. The sounds of bones crunching and blood spurting reverberate through the streets. Kevin soars to Tristan, scooping up his lifeless body in his arms, and all of them disappear in a gush of smoke before I can launch another attack.

Crouching down beside Eli, he is still unconscious; his breathing is shallow. His face is pale and twisted in agony from his broken arm. I gently place my hand on his chest, conjuring my magic to heal his injuries.

Heal.

Nothing happens.

Heal.

Still nothing.

Mr. Max, Mr. Goatfair, and Lin bolt toward us, transferring their magic into me, and I try again. I'm able to heal his arm, but he is still unconscious.

"Why isn't he waking up?" I look to everyone around me for answers, except no one has any.

Cradling Eli in my arms, tears stream down my face as I fear the worst. I hug him tight, hoping he will wake up and be okay. Still, the surrounding silence is deafening, broken only by the sound of my sobs.

This means war!

Chapter 13

Fated Lovers

"Please help me take him inside," I beg.

Lin and Mr. Max gently lift Eli's limp body from my arms and carry him into the apartment. I follow closely behind, the sound of shuffling feet filling the air as everyone else mimics my movements. As we gently place him on the bed, his face remains pale and motionless.

"What do we do now?" I ask.

Everyone exchanges uneasy glances.

The silence stretches on, and my anger bubbles to the surface. "Someone, please answer me!"

"There is nothing more we can do but wait," Lin says.

Wait for him to wake up or die?

Waves of shivers run through my body, and I instinctively clutch my elbows to steady myself. "I—I thought I healed him. Why isn't he waking up?" My voice cracks, and a ripple of emotions threatens to overwhelm me.

Ms. Caron's eyes fill with empathy. "You healed him physically. He was struck by magical fireballs, which will take time to recover from."

"H—how long?"

Ms. Caron bends down to Eli's still form, gently rubbing the back of her hand on his forehead. "It's hard to say. Hours, days, maybe even weeks." She says.

I watch over Eli's unconscious body. Ms. Caron's words repeat in my mind. *Hours, days, maybe even weeks.* There is no telling if or when he will wake up.

"We need to prepare for war in the meantime," Mr. Goatfair adds. "Kevin only gave us a taste of his powers. They'll be back stronger next time, especially since Claudette killed that little worm."

"Let's discuss strategies," Destiny suggests, and they gather in the living room, leaving me alone with Eli and Lin.

Sitting beside Eli, I hold his hand tight, hoping for a miracle.

"Anything you need, just let us know," Lin offers.

"There's one thing you can do," I say.

Lin looks at me expectantly, waiting for my request.

"What is Eli's favorite meal?"

Confusion spreads across his face as he processes my odd question. Still, he recovers and responds, "Uh, he loves pasta and seafood."

A plan forms in my mind. "Did Eli tell you where he took me when he told me Kevin had something to do with my father's death?"

Lin pauses, trying to recall the memory. "Ah, yes. He took you to his secret hideout."

Secret?

"How do I get there?" I ask, picking at Lin's brain.

When Eli wakes up, I want to plan a surprise that will leave him speechless.

"Caron can make a potion for a portal. If you remember what the place looks like, you can portal there."

"You wouldn't be able to take me there? Or can't I just portal there on my own?" I lift an eyebrow.

Lin shakes his head. "No, Claudette. I have no idea what Eli's hideout looks like, and I don't think it's in this realm, which is why you would need a potion." He looks down at his best friend's unconscious body. "Eli really loves you, you know. He never takes anyone there." With that, Lin gives me a nod and exits the room to join the others in the living room, leaving me to ponder his words.

After undressing Eli into something more comfortable, I settle down by his side.

The blame falls on me. I was the distraction that led Eli to this state. My heart is heavy with guilt as I watch him lie there. All he ever tried to do was warn me about Kevin, and now he's paying the price for my negligence. I was madly in lust with that demon—because that wasn't love—and I failed to see the danger Eli was trying to protect me from. *I wish I had listened to him sooner.* A deep sadness overcomes me, causing tears to well up in my eyes.

Kevin is now unrecognizable. His once charming features have crumbled, revealing the monster beneath. He glared at me with pitch-black eyes and a sinister grin. The red horns that protruded from his head made my blood turn to ice. How was I ever in love with such evil? *I was in lust, not love.*

A knock on the door distracts me from my inner thoughts.

"Come in," I call out, wiping away my tears.

The door creaks open, and Ms. Caron enters with two potion bottles in her hands. "This one is a protection spell for the apartment while Eli heals. It will time out in seventy-two hours, and I will give you another one if necessary," she explains, placing the first bottle on the nightstand. "This one is for a portal," she adds, positioning the second bottle next to the first with a reassuring smile. "Sweetie, listen to me. You are extremely powerful, and you have the strength to defeat Kevin. Still, you have to learn to channel the Earth's energy and the love that surrounds you when accessing your powers. Or it will destroy you."

"Thank you for the advice, Ms. Caron." I smile up at her. "And thank you so much for the potions. When did you have the time to make them?"

She cackles. "I have a bookshelf full of ready-made potions."

The cackling is peculiar, but I appreciate the potions that she has provided me with.

"I really appreciate you supplying me with both of these potions, Ms. Caron."

"Oh, honey, it's no trouble at all," she winks. "And you can call me Caron. We are not in school. No need to be so formal."

"Thank you, *Caron*," I correct.

Mr. Goatfair peeks his head into the room. "May I speak with you, Claudette?"

Caron turns her attention to Mr. Goatfair. "I was just leaving, Adam. She's all yours," she says, exiting the room.

He sits on the edge of the bed beside me.

"What do you need to speak to me about, Mr. Goatfair?" My brows furrow.

He raises his hand to stop me from speaking. "Adam is fine."

Clearing my throat, I start over. "Alright, *Adam*, what did you want to talk about?"

He looks at me with a serious expression. "We're one of the last Earth witches left in this town. You, me, Jessie, and Lin."

"My father left me a letter on a flash drive," I admit, and Adam nods knowingly. "He told me to reach out to you or Jimmy. Why would he tell me that?"

"Chance told me he would explain everything to you, but he was taken before he could." Adam's expression softens as he continues, "Your father knew there was danger coming, and he wanted to make sure you were prepared. He trusts me to help guide you in the right direction. Do you have your Earth book?"

"No. My father hid it in a safe place in the house, but I don't have the key. We need to find his necklace; it was stolen the night he was murdered."

Adam's mouth forms a small O. "We can do a locator spell to find it, but I need something of his for it to work."

"I don't want to go back to the house he was killed in, Adam. Please don't make me." I plead with him.

Adam nods in understanding. "I will figure something out with Caron, Billie, and Jessie. We will get you what you need. Even if it's a bit unorthodox." He says, rubbing his fingers together.

I give him a small smile. "Thank you, Adam."

Adam gives me a slight grin before turning to leave the room. "We are calling it a night. Rest up, kid, and let us know when Eli wakes up."

It is three in the morning when everyone leaves. The protection spell Caron casts will ward off any unwanted visitors, which also means Eli and I can't leave the premises unless through a portal.

I curl up on the soft, cozy bed next to Eli, hoping that the soothing rhythm of his breathing will lull me to sleep as I silently pray for a brighter tomorrow.

Upon waking up the following morning, Eli's condition remains the same. Throughout the night, I periodically woke up to check on him, hoping he would wake up. As the hours passed, my anxiety grew. *I don't know what to do.* My stomach growls with hunger. I haven't eaten since yesterday morning, so I head to the kitchen to make some breakfast. I quickly prepare some scrambled eggs and plop down on the sofa to eat. Despite my hunger, I struggle to swallow each bite. I feel helpless. My heart feels empty, and there is a void that can only be filled by my best friend.

Four hours of watching old sitcoms and movies on Netflix pass by in a blur. The apartment feels empty without Eli's usual banter and laughter filling the space. I drag my feet to the bathroom to shower and get dressed, but even a shower doesn't seem to wash away the emptiness I feel without my best friend around. I skim through Eli's Moon book, looking for something—anything that can help wake him up. As I mindlessly flip through the pages, I remember the flash drive my father had left me. There was a folder labeled *Fated Lovers*. I check on Eli once more to ensure he's still breathing, then grab the flash drive and plug it into my laptop. I open the folder and begin reading through the documents.

It states that fated lovers are two souls destined to find each other in every lifetime and bound to merge their magic to be the most powerful beings in the world. The merging spell that Eli cast on us is listed here. This spell is for all fated lovers—Sun, Moon, or Earth—to perform in order to unlock their full potential. *"Confess one's true self."* The bottom of the document reads. *What does that mean?* Confess one's true self. I repeat the phrase in my head, trying to decipher its meaning. Then it hits me—it was always Eli. *Not* Kevin. The sight of his true demon nature was the final push I needed to let him go and fully embrace my destiny with Eli. I had been suppressing my true feelings for him this entire time, never truly admitting how I felt about him.

Ejecting the flash drive, I hasten to Eli's room. Straddling his motionless body, I whisper, "Eli, I love you with all my heart and accept you as my mate." Electricity courses between us, and I press my lips to his, savoring the taste of destiny fulfilled. "Eli," I say softly, "I love you in every lifetime, in every universe. I confess my true feelings to you. I accept our fate. Do you accept me?" I wait with bated breaths for his response. Still, he remains motionless, his eyes closed.

"Please, Eli. Please wake up. I need you here with me. Please don't leave me alone in this world without you." I kiss his forehead, both sides of his face, and his lips, hoping to bring him back to me. Still, there is no response from him. My tears fall onto his cheeks as I plead for him to come back to me. "I need my best friend. Please wake up, Eli." I press my face against his well-defined chest, inhaling his familiar scent. I feel his faint heartbeat beneath my cheek. "I can't do this without you," I whisper, clinging to the belief that he will open his eyes, except he doesn't. *What will it take for him to wake up?* I confessed my feelings for him. How else can I show him how much he means to me?

EARTH

Standing up, I quickly draw in a deep breath, allowing my lungs to fill with air. In an effort to convey my deep affection for him, I conjure a sphere that captures all my love. The orb shimmers with white illumination. Vivid memories of our time together flood my mind, causing the orb to shine and intensify. I have doubts about its effectiveness; however, I release it into the air. The luminous sphere hovers over Eli's body, emanating warmth and love. My hands tremble as I guide the orb above his heart. Eli's chest rises and falls, synchronized with the ethereal orb's rhythm. The transference of light from the vessel into his body ascends him toward the ceiling. Floating in mid-air, he emits a radiant glow before settling back onto the bed. The luminescence fades, and his eyes flutter open. He blinks a few times, taking in his surroundings.

"Eli! You're awake!" I shriek.

Clearing his throat, "Yeah, it seems like it. What happened?"

Leaping onto the bed, I straddle him.

"You have been unconscious for over fifteen hours," I tell him.

"Yet, I feel exhausted," he says, instinctively grasping my waist.

"Do you remember what happened?"

He shakes his head slowly, a puzzled expression on his face. "What happened?"

I recount the events that led to his unconsciousness, my eyes filled with tears. "You were knocked out by a magical fireball. How are you feeling?"

He listens intently, his expression shifting from confusion to amusement. "Fifteen hours?" he repeats. "I still feel exhausted."

Cracking a small smile. "You had us all worried sick," I admit, embracing him. "Don't do that again, okay?"

Eli chuckles. "Perhaps I should be knocked unconscious more often."

Pushing him back with my fist. "No! Don't do that to me again, okay?" Biting my bottom lip. "I—I love you so much, Eli. I don't know what I would do without you—I wouldn't survive without you."

His eyes soften, and his hand reaches up to wipe away a stray tear from my cheek. "I love you too, more than you'll ever know," he says with a sincerity that warms my heart. But you don't *need* me to survive."

I look at him, my brows furrowed in confusion. "What do you mean?"

Eli's lips curve into a sexy smile. "I mean that you are strong and capable on your own. I'll always be here for you, but we are not meant to live in this realm forever. If something were to happen to me, you would have the strength to survive, and I will be waiting for you in the Light World."

I don't want to think about life without him.

Sliding off of Eli, I lower myself onto the floor, my face reflecting a sense of seriousness.

He sits up on the bed, his eyes locked on me with a guarded expression. "Claudette?"

Savoring the intimate moment, I deliberately lower my shorts, feeling the material slide against my skin. Eli's eyes flicker with intrigue, and my gaze shifts to the pulsating bulge in his sweatpants.

Lost in the moment, I move closer to him without realizing that I didn't properly remove my shorts. As a result, I trip over the fabric and awkwardly land on the floor, the impact creating a soft thud. My cheeks flush with embarrassment, causing me to instinctively bury my face against the coolness of the tiles. In a matter of seconds, the atmosphere transitions from intimate to awkward. I wish the Earth would open up and swallow me whole, sparing me from this unbearable situation.

Eli peers down at me. "Claudette?"

"Yes?" I mumble, my voice muffled by the tiles.

"Are you okay?"

"I think I'll stay down here for a while."

He chuckles softly, crouching down beside me. "Let me help you up."

Exhaling a deep breath, I accept his offer and regain my footing. My gaze meets his, and we share a knowing look before bursting into laughter and falling back onto the bed. The awkwardness fades away, and when our laughter eases, he cocks his head to the side. "What are we?"

"We're fated lovers," I reply with a smile.

"No, Claudette."

My smile fades. *No?*

"You're sitting on my bed half-naked," he clarifies with a smirk, leaning in closer.

My breath catches in my throat. Just being near Elijah Powers is enough to make me lose all strength in my limbs.

His hand slowly slides up my thigh, and a rush of heat courses through my body. "What are we?" he asks again, his warm breath tickling my skin.

"We are one," I reply breathlessly.

His eyes lock onto mine, a dashing smile playing on his lips as a silent understanding passes between us.

"What do you want from me, Claudette?" His voice is low and husky.

My throat tightens, and I gulp nervously. "I—I want all of you."

He traces delicate kisses down my collarbone. "What do you need from me, Claudette?"

When he touches me, it feels like a surge of electricity, causing a tingling sensation all over my body.

"I need all of you," I reply; my pulse quickens as his touch sends shivers down my spine. "Eli, I want you to be with me in all ways possible. I am yours, and I love you."

With a seductive grin, he removes his shirt, showcasing his chiseled chest and toned muscles. My mouth is watering as I am unable to contain my admiration for his flawless physique.

He gently pulls my shirt over my head and unhooks my bra, momentarily leaving me disoriented. His gaze hungrily takes in every inch of my exposed skin.

"Do you want me to make love to you, Claudette?"

"Yes, please," I mutter, my body trembling with anticipation.

He quickly stands to his feet and kicks off his sweatpants and boxers, leaving nothing to the imagination, exposing his entire length to me.

Our eyes lock in a passionate gaze as he retrieves protection from the drawer and carefully slides it on. My jaw drops in awe, and he responds with a wide, toothy grin that brightens his entire face.

I love Eli with every fiber of my being, and I want to show him just how much. I reach out to him, grab his arm, and pull him back onto the bed. Adrenaline courses through my veins as I slide off my underwear and straddle him. "I love you, Elijah Powers."

He grips my hips firmly. "I love you, Claudette Richardson."

Lowering myself onto him, I bite my bottom lip to stifle a moan as our bodies become one. Eli groans softly, claiming my lips with his own in a passionate kiss. His hands explore every inch of my body as I rock my hips in rhythm with his. He whispers sweet nothings in my ear, caressing my skin with kisses and leaving a trail of fire in his wake. Our breathing is heavy, intermingling with the sound of the mattress creaking beneath us.

Eli grasps me by the waist and flips us over, taking control.

Every kiss feels like a drug.

Every touch intoxicates my senses, bringing me to the brink of ecstasy. With each thrust, our passion intensifies as I arch my back to meet his every movement. My body quivers with jolts of pleasure, and I grip the sheets. I have never experienced anything quite like this before. It's pure bliss in every sense. The intensity of Eli's thrusts escalates, sending waves of pleasure coursing through our bodies. In a fleeting moment, my body transcends into a fit of euphoria, and I am transported to a realm of pure bliss. As I come down from the height of passion, I can feel his body trembling with anticipation, leading up to his climax. Overwhelmed with exhaustion, we both collapse, panting and basking in the joyful aftermath of our passionate lovemaking.

I thought that when I lost my virginity to Kevin, we were making love, but I couldn't have been more wrong. What Eli and I shared was more than just physical intimacy.

It was two souls merging as one.

Chapter 14

All is Revealed

My eyes flicker open, and I look to my left and admire Eli. Resting my head on his chiseled chest, listening to his steady heartbeat against my ear, his warm breath on my neck—it feels like home. This handsome man told me he loved me and showed me just how much he did last night. He was attentive to what my body needed and made sure I felt pleasure from every touch. My desire is to show him just how much I appreciate him.

I roll over to grab my phone on the nightstand and text Lin to come over to help distract Eli while I work on my surprise for him.

Leaning back, Eli meets my gaze, grinning from ear to ear.

"Good morning, Sunshine."

Returning his smile, I move closer to him and kiss him on the lips. "Good morning, baby. Would you like me to make you some breakfast?"

"So, this is the *girlfriend* Claudette treatment?" Eli teases, making me laugh.

Shoving him playfully. "I love the sound of being your girlfriend."

"Me too," he replies, pressing his lips against mine again.

"I'll make you some after my shower." I get up from the bed, but he pulls me back down, wrapping his muscular arms around me and holding me firmly in his grasp.

Melting into his embrace, I feel safe and loved in his arms. Feeling his frame against mine sends a comforting sensation throughout my entire body. Eli is different from Kevin. Thinking back, the whole time Kevin and I were intimate, he seemed distant and unengaged. While with Eli, he was present and attentive. Suddenly, guilt washes over me, weighing heavy on my conscience for comparing the two. I shouldn't be. Still, Eli is the second guy I've been with, and I can't help but notice the stark contrast between them.

Tracing my fingers along Eli's eight-pack. "Babe, I have to brush my teeth."

"Yeah, you do. Your breath stinks," he jokes, giving me a quick peck on the lips.

I playfully throw a pillow at his head. "Shut up. So does yours."

He chuckles, blowing out his stinky breath on my face. *Wow! I love him.*

Opening and closing the cabinets, I am trying to figure out what to make Eli for breakfast. Kevin usually cooked for me, and now that I think about it, he used his culinary skills to win me over and manipulate me. *That demon!* However, Eli is *not* Kevin. From the moment we met, there was a genuine connection between us—an unexplainable pull that defied logic. We are destined to be together. *Why didn't I just trust my instincts from the start?*

Opting for my father's famous buttermilk pancakes, I gather the ingredients and start whipping up a batch. Twenty minutes later, breakfast is ready. I place the pancakes onto the table and pour orange juice into two flutes.

Eli walks in shirtless, wearing gray sweatpants. "Breakfast smells good."

He is so sexy.

"It's my dad's infamous buttermilk pancakes," I reply gleefully.

His muscles ripple as he sits down at the table to dig in. I anxiously await his reaction, butterflies fluttering in my stomach.

"These are great, babe," he compliments between bites. "What did I do to deserve you?"

My smile falters slightly as guilt creeps in. "I am sorry it took me so long to reciprocate your feelings," I confess, looking down at my plate.

Eli reaches across the table, gently lifting my chin. "You were worth the wait," he says, making my heart skip a beat. "I am happy that we are here now."

We enjoy our breakfast, engaging in light conversation and sharing laughs.

Ring. Ring.

My phone interrupts our playful banter.

Caron is calling me. Back to reality: I answer the call with a sigh. She, Billie, and Adam are heading to my dad's house to steal something of his to perform the locater spell to find his Earth necklace and, hopefully, his ring, too.

Eli is loading the dishwasher when I end the call, and I quickly fill him in.

"My father left me a flash drive with important information about my family history, including the location of his Earth book. However, his Earth necklace and ring are missing. I need his necklace to unlock the box the book is in. Caron, Billie, and Adam are on their way to my dad's house to find something of his so that we can conduct a locator spell to find his Earth ring and necklace."

Eli nods in understanding and offers to help in any way he can.

When silence falls between us, he changes the subject to steer me away from gnawing over the situation. "What would you like to do today as an official couple?"

Smiling at the sound of the title *couple*. "I actually have something planned for us."

"Oh! You do?" He arches his brow.

As I nod my head, a bubbling excitement rises in my chest, like a sparkling drink ready to burst. "Yes, however, afterward, everyone is coming over to conduct the spell to locate my father's necklace." I say once again.

Eli squeezes my hand. "I'm here for you, whatever you need."

A knock sounds at the door, interrupting our moment.

Eli goes to answer it. Lin enters with a huge smile on his face, pulling Eli in for a bear hug. "I'm so happy you are awake. My brother!"

"I will give you two some time to catch up," I say, kissing Eli on the cheek.

Lin points between the two of us. "Oh! Are you two a thing now?" He asks, sporting a huge grin.

I wink at him before heading out of the room.

Rummaging through Eli's closet, I search for a blanket for our date later. I find a soft, cozy blanket and head to my room for supplies. I gather a crochet hook, some gold yarn, and scissors to crochet an E and C into the blanket.

Caron temporarily deactivated the protection spell to permit Eli to leave the apartment with Lin. I use the opportunity to cook a delicious meal for our date, opting for shrimp Alfredo, knowing that Eli's favorite dish is pasta and seafood. I pack the food into containers and into a basket with a blanket and a bottle of sparkling cider. With the potion Caron had given me securely in my grasp, I set my sights on embarking on a journey to Eli's secret haven. In this place, we can fully immerse ourselves in the breathtaking beauty of the sunset as we stand atop the highest point of the mountain.

Eli returns to the apartment just in time for our date, and I go to greet him. My smile falters when I notice the deep frown etched on his face.

"What's wrong, babe?"

"You killed Tristan, Claudette?" He asks, his eyes searching mine for answers.

Despite my reluctance, I lower my gaze to my feet and reply, "Yes, I did. I didn't know what else to do. There was rage brewing inside me, and I couldn't control my anger."

Eli's expression changes. His features relax, and his gaze softens as he reaches out to hold my hand. "The angrier you become, the faster your powers will deplete."

Sighing, I look down at our intertwined hands. "Caron told me to access my power from the Earth's energy and the love that surrounds me."

"Yes, that's correct. Access your power by channeling it from the Earth and the love you have for your parents, me, and your friends." Eli encourages me. "You have been filled with rage and anger every time you have used your power." He points out.

"How do I protect those I love if killing isn't the way to do it?"

Eli's eyes hold understanding. "Killing is the last resort, Claudette. You can protect your loved ones by using your power to defend, not destroy."

When I find out who killed my father, I plan to return the favor by executing them. I keep that thought to myself and smile. Retrieving my phone from my pocket, I send Spencer and Nicolette a text, informing them of everything.

Looking up at Eli. "I can't believe Kevin is evil and killed Jimmy."

"I expected nothing less; he is a demon, after all." He replies.

Putting my phone away, I place my hands on both sides of Eli's shoulders and look him straight in the eyes. He grasps my waist, his expression filled with concern. Taking a deep breath in and letting it out slowly, I focus on releasing the tension in my body.

"Let's not worry about our reality right now." I smile, trying to lighten the mood. "I have a surprise for you, babe."

His grip on my waist tightens. "I'm intrigued."

"You should be," I reply, pushing away from him before we get too distracted. I lead him by the hand to get the basket I had prepared and the potion bottle.

Eli raises an eyebrow in curiosity, his gaze shifting between the basket and the potion in my hands.

"You'll see soon enough," I assure him with a playful grin.

Closing my eyes, I envision the day Eli took me to the mountains. Shattering the potion bottle on the floor, I whisper, "Take me to Eli's secret spot."

The potion's effects take hold, and we transport to the mountain peak. Watching Eli's face light up as he recognizes the familiar view brings a warm feeling to my heart.

Breathing in the fresh mountain air, I unpack the basket and present the blanket crocheted with our initials. Eli's eyes widen in amazement as he carefully traces over my craftsmanship with his fingertips, a smile spreading across his face. "This is incredible, babe," he murmurs, pulling me into a tight hug.

We spread out the blanket and settle in, taking in the mesmerizing waterfall. *Just as I remember it.* Unpacking the pasta and sparkling cider, Eli pours us each a glass, and I feed him a bite of pasta. His eyes light up with delight, and he pulls me into his muscular arms. "I love you, Claudette." He kisses me as if it were our last.

I don't think I'll ever grow tired of hearing those three words from him.

"I love you too, Eli," I reply against his full lips.

He grins. "It's about time. It took you long enough."

"Oh, shush." I playfully slap his chest. "I have always had a thing for you since we first met," I confess. "I guess I was just in denial about it."

Eli embraces me tighter. "Well, I'm glad you finally came to your senses," he teases, making me laugh. "I like to believe that things happen when they're meant to. And this moment feels just right."

Eli leans in to kiss me again, his lips soft and warm against mine, but before things can go any further, we pull away to finish our dinner. We enjoy each other's company and conversation. Once we are done with our meal, we marvel at the sunset, painting the sky in an array of colors.

"Thank you, babe," he says, looking me in the eye. "For everything."

I smile, staring into his eyes. "You're welcome."

Enveloped in the beauty of the evening and consumed by the warmth of his love, Eli's sensual kiss ignites a passionate fire within me, and we find ourselves connecting beneath the breathtaking red and orange hues of the setting sun. Reflecting on the gradual buildup of our love, I can't help but wonder what it would have been like if I had met him first—the thought consumes me.

Ding.

I glance at my phone, and it is a text from Lin. He and the others are on their way to meet us at the apartment.

"It's time to go, baby. Back to reality." I tell Eli as we reluctantly untangle ourselves from each other. We gather our clothes from the ground and quickly get dressed. We pack the basket to head back to the apartment, where Lin, Caron, Adam, and Billie are waiting for us. Eli transports us back to the apartment in a flash.

Everyone is in the living room when we arrive, surrounding the table. Caron lights a candle and places the town map in the center. "Gabriella didn't give me a hard time when I went to your father's house. She agrees the twins have lost their minds and are not acting like themselves, and she doesn't know what to do. We chatted for a bit, and when she went to make us some tea, I snuck away to grab this ring from their bedroom," Caron explains, holding up a gold band.

"How were you able to go upstairs to their bedroom without her noticing?"

She cackles, "A lady never reveals her secrets." *Caron loves to cackle, I notice.* Tilting her head to the side, Caron adds, "The better question would be, is this your father's wedding band?"

Inspecting the gold band in her hand, I nod my head.

Adam joins us with a bowl, burdock root, and grass. Caron pours a bottled potion carefully into the bowl, making sure not to spill a single drop, and then delicately drops the gold ring into the mixture. A gray smoke billows from the bowl, and she skillfully wields a baster to extract the liquid that has formed. She then squirts the liquid onto the map.

"The locations of your father's possessions will be revealed," Adam explains.

We all watch in anticipation as the liquid slowly begins to spread across the map, dividing into two distinct locations.

Kevin's apartment. And Ms. Hudson's home.

My trust shatters like glass, and I swiftly retrieve my father's ring from the bowl.

Everyone's eyes widen as they exchange uneasy glances. *Is Ms. Hudson involved in my father's death?* My vision blurs with an overwhelming darkness, and an impenetrable sense of rage consumes me entirely.

"Wait! Claudette, don't leave!" Caron shouts.

"Claudette!" Eli yells, echoing Caron's plea.

Ignoring them both, I slam the door behind me.

The mere thought of Ms. Hudson's house triggers a magical teleportation. In an instant, I materialize in front of her doorstep.

Remaining calm, I ball up my fist and knock on the door, patiently waiting for her to answer.

The door swings open, and Ms. Hudson's eyebrows furrow in confusion. "Hello, Claudette. Did we have a session today?"

I direct my gaze straight into her eyes. *How could she help me cope with my father's death when she was the very person responsible for it?*

Forging a smile, I push down the rage bubbling inside me and politely respond, "No, Ms. Hudson. I just wanted to talk. May I come in?"

"Sure, sweetie, come on in." She gestures for me to enter her office.

I follow her inside, a flurry of fiery emotions swirling inside me.

"Please take a seat," Ms. Hudson says, motioning to the chair in front of her desk.

"No, I'd rather stand," I reply, unable to bring myself to sit down in front of the woman who shattered my world.

Clutching the ring in my hand, I pace back and forth. She opens the drawer of her desk to retrieve her notebook and pen to begin our unplanned session.

She opens her notebook, looking at me expectantly. "So, tell me.

Claudette, what's been going on?"

There's a storm brewing inside me, and I know that once I start talking, there will be no turning back. "I know you like to stay out of witch business, but Kevin attacked my friends and me. He is evil."

Ms. Hudson fake gasps. "Oh no, that's terrible, Claudette! I had no idea. I'm sorry to hear that. Were you, or were your friends hurt? Is that why you are here today?" She pulls out her calendar and continues. "I know we weren't supposed to meet until next week."

She is lying through her teeth. It is remarkable how effortlessly she can pretend. What an incredible actress! She deserves an award! *Was it all an act to get me to trust her and open up?*

Walking closer to her. "Yes and no," I reply.

Ms. Hudson tilts her head slightly, waiting for me to continue.

My mind deliberates over the various spells at my disposal. "Turn the darkness into light, reveal the truth, and give me sight." My voice takes on a sinister edge as I chant this spell three times, the intensity building with each iteration.

The witch's eyes widen in despair, and she jumps to her feet. "W–what are you doing?" She stammers.

A visible light shines inside her drawer, and the color drains from her face. She quickly moves out of my way, and I find my father's Earth ring stashed inside, nestled under her notebooks from our sessions.

I collect the ring and play with it in my palm. Cocking my head to the side. "You see, this ring is why I am here today," I tell her calmly, holding up the ring for her to see. "Why do you have my father's ring, Ms. Hudson?" Fear flashes in her eyes, and a malicious grin spreads across my face. "Are you scared now, Ms. Hudson?"

"N–no. Why would I fear you?" She stammers, her shaky voice exposing her nervousness.

Because you should be. I catch a glimpse of my reflection in the small mirror on her desk. The darkness within me is reflected in the blackness of my eyes, a side of myself that I never believed existed.

With deliberate steps, I approach her. "Why did you do it?"

Her answer won't change her fate, but I derive a certain satisfaction from watching her squirm.

"Why did I do what, Claudette?" Ms. Hudson quivers under my gaze, feigning innocence.

"You know exactly what I'm talking about!" She flinches at my accusatory tone. "You killed my father!"

A painful recognition crosses her face. "I had no choice, Claudette. I am so sorry," she apologizes, her voice wavering with guilt.

A lousy sorry won't bring my father back. Extending my arm, I summon a fiery red fireball, feeling its warmth against my skin as it takes form in my hand.

Ms. Hudson's eyes widen, and a look of sheer horror flashes across her face. "Please, Claudette, I beg you, please don't do this," she pleads, her voice desperate.

Eli specifically emphasized the importance of not channeling my rage. Shaking off his warning, it's too late for mercy. All I feel is rage in its purest form, consuming me from the inside out. This lady—*my therapist*—convinced me to open up about my trauma, only to team up with Kevin and kill my father. That is the epitome of wickedness. Evil like that deserves to be met with an equal measure of inhumanity.

"Why did you kill my father?" I demand, playing with the fireball in my hand.

Her eyes dart at its fiery glow. "I...I..."

The flames flicker dangerously, and I shake my head at her incoherent stammering. "I...I...*What?*"

"I–I didn't have a choice. I–I swear it," she chokes out.

I scoff at her weak excuse. "Wrong answer." With a swift motion, I aim the fireball precisely at her heart, striking her with unforgiving force. She falls off balance, collapsing to the floor with a pained cry. As she writhes in agony, she conjures a fireball of her own, and with the last of her strength, she hurls it at me. It doesn't even sting. *She is pathetic.*

As I ascend above her, a malicious smirk forms on my face at her feeble pleas. I want this witch to suffer.

"Claudette, please don't do this," she begs, tears streaming down her face. "I didn't have a choice."

She will say just about anything to save herself, but she didn't spare any mercy for my father when she took his life.

"You had a choice, Ms. Hudson, or is it *Libby?*" I snort. "You chose to betray me. Now deal with the consequences of *your* actions!"

My lips curve into a malicious grin as I start breaking the twenty-six bones in her right foot, relishing in her screams of pain. Her anguish fills me with a twisted sense of delight as I break the bones in her other foot.

"Please..." she manages to say.

I proceed to break the bones in her legs, and she falls in and out of consciousness, her body battered and broken, as I carry out her fate. I heal her and break all her bones again. Repeating the process over and over again.

"Please... Claudette... Stop..." Her voice is barely a whisper now.

Even after she committed the heinous act of killing my father in cold blood, she had the nerve to still act as my therapist. I have no sympathy for her! She brought this upon herself.

I continue to fracture every bone in her body—the cracks echoing in my ears like sickening symphonies—inflicting bruising, bleeding, and irreversible deformation. I heal her just enough to keep her alive, prolonging her suffering for as long as possible. A quick death would be too merciful for her.

Her whimpers are hoarse and barely audible now, begging for mercy that will never come. When I grow tired of her torment and incessant pleas, I regard her with a cold, unsympathetic gaze and say, "Any last words? Witch?" I ask, raising her above me toward the ceiling.

She opens her mouth to speak, but strangled cries escape her lips as I seal her fate with a snap of my fingers, fatally breaking her neck. The life drains from the witch's eyes, and her limp body falls to the hard floor, lifeless and broken.

I glide toward her and lower my ear near her body. "I'm sorry, I didn't hear you."

Stepping over her motionless body, I open and close my hands, torching her residence and leaving nothing but charred remains behind.

Chapter 15

Consumed by Rage

The moment I appear at the apartment, the room starts to spin, and I feel drained of all energy, causing me to collapse to the ground.

Several hours later...

What happened? As I slowly regain consciousness, a wave of dizziness hits me, making it difficult to focus. In the background, I can hear faint voices murmuring, but I'm unsure of whose voice belongs to whom.

A hazy figure looms over me. My vision is blurred, making it hard to see their features; however, I immediately recognize their scent. *Eli!*

"Claudette," Eli calls out, shaking me gently. "Are you okay? Can you hear me?"

I try to focus on his words, yet everything sounds distant. *Why can't I see clearly?* My head is pounding, and there is a throbbing sensation behind my eyes.

"Claudette, can you hear us?" Another voice joins in. I attempt to reply, but my mouth feels dry as a desert, yearning for raindrops from the sky. *Why can't I move or speak?*

The tightness in my chest intensifies, making each breath a struggle. Despite my best efforts, I strain to open my heavy and unresponsive eyes. *What's happening to me?* The voices in the background call my name and echo in my ears until everything goes silent. The world around me fades to black, accompanied by swirling white spots in my vision as I succumb to unconsciousness once again.

Eli's point of view:

Kneeling beside Claudette's sleeping form on the sofa, my fingers tremble as I reach out to touch her clammy skin. Even in her vulnerable state, her beauty is enhanced by the gentle rise and fall of her chest as she breathes. I shake her gently, calling out her name. Still, she remains unresponsive. Panic takes hold of my heart, squeezing it tight. Kevin and his minions are expected to retaliate soon, and Claudette is not waking up. *What do I do?* A sense of urgency sets in as I frantically shake her, but she shows no signs of waking. Her breathing is steady and her pulse is strong, but she is lost in a deep slumber.

"What are we going to do now?" I shout to no one in particular. "Claudette killed Ms. Hudson. It is only a matter of time before Kevin shows up."

Claudette has already killed two of their own. Kevin will not take that lightly, and we need to prevent him from finding out Claudette is unconscious.

Caron steadies me by squeezing my shoulders. "Eli, she is drained. There is nothing more we can do. She has to wake up on her own."

Nothing? I shift my gaze towards Claudette, and my shoulders sink in defeat. Carefully, I cradle Claudette in my arms and gently transfer her to the comfort of my bed, ensuring she is tucked in with a soft, warm blanket.

Brushing her locs away from her face, anguish settles in my chest. If only I had taken the necessary precautions, maybe this could have been avoided. We should have been better prepared. I suspected Claudette would react emotionally when she found her father's killer. She was shocked and devastated. The revelation hit her like a ton of bricks—her therapist was the murderer all along, and none of us saw it coming. This blindsided me, and I can only imagine how much more it affected Claudette. *What did Kevin have on Ms. Hudson?* There must have been some sort of leverage he had over Ms. Hudson to manipulate her into doing his bidding. I always knew Kevin was evil, but *Ms. Hudson?* She and Jimmy were the only two members of the Witch Council that I didn't hate. Now, Jimmy, Ms. Hudson, and Tristan are dead. Claudette's father is dead. And all the Earth witches sacrificed for Kevin's ritual. *How many more lives need to be lost in this fight?*

Allowing Claudette to rest, I return to the living room, pacing back and forth. Everyone exchanges worried glances. *Think, Eli. Think.* Claudette is a good witch, yet she keeps channeling rage to harness her magic. She won't listen to reason, especially now that she's lost so much. However, there must be a way to reach her. *I got it!*

I barge into Claudette's room, my eyes scanning the space for something specific among her belongings. What am I looking for? I don't know yet. *How can I help her channel love and not rage?*

There it is—I spot her laptop on her desk; I quickly grab it and open it. It's password-protected, and I need four numeric digits to unlock it. I try a few common passwords, like her birthday and her dad's birthday. Luckily, she has the obituary sitting on her shelf. However, none of them work. I only have one more attempt left before the laptop locks me out. Tapping my fingers on the desk, I rack my brain for any other numbers that could be significant to her. I try my birthday, typing in 0-3-1-7, and to my surprise, the laptop unlocks. I smile, shaking my head. *I love this girl.* Claudette informed me that her father left her a flash drive; perhaps there is something on there that could help wake her up or at least speed up the process. Where would

Claudette hide a flash drive? Closing my eyes, I gesture my hands around the room, focusing my mind on the object. "I call upon the moon of the night; give me a clear vision and sight. Reveal to me what my heart desires; reveal to me what I might require." I chant.

Claudette's mattress is bathed in a dazzling light, emanating an incredible and exquisite glow. Lifting it up, I find what I need. Her jewelry box. The flash drive is safely tucked away inside of it. Plugging in the drive, a series of files and folders appear on the screen. I groan internally. It will take hours, maybe days, to go through all of this.

I begin the long process of sifting through the folders on her laptop. Still, after forty minutes of searching, I stop to rub the bridge of my nose, feeling a headache coming on. Scrolling through more files, I exhale when I stumble across a spell that permits people from the Light World to crossover. I write down the spell on a piece of paper and close the laptop, returning the flash drive to its original spot.

Heading to my room, I check on Claudette, who is still knocked out on the bed. Closing the door behind me, I make my way to the living room to find Caron talking with Adam, who is listening intently.

"Hi, have you ever done this spell before?" I politely interrupt them, showing them my scribbles on the paper.

She takes the paper from my hand and studies it carefully before shaking her head. "No," she says, glancing at Adam.

"I have done this spell before with Chance." He clears his throat. "He wanted to speak to his, um, Claudette's mother."

"Do you think it could wake Claudette up?" I ask.

Caron and Adam exchange a knowing look before Caron replies, "I don't think so, sweetie."

"Her father left this spell for her as a way to see him again," Adam adds. "The spell is for speaking with the dead." He continues.

A heavy sense of hopelessness engulfs me, making it hard to breathe. *What now?* Kevin is plotting. It is only a matter of time before he makes his move.

"There has to be something we can do!" I shout.

Caron, Lin, Adam, and Billie watch me warily as I pace back and forth.

Now that the roles are reversed, I can empathize with how Claudette felt when I was unconscious. *This sucks!*

"How did Claudette wake you up?" Lin inquires.

I stop pacing and turn to face him. *I have no idea how she woke me up.* I remember feeling an overpowering sensation of warmth and light, but beyond that, it's all a blur. It felt like she was channeling all her love into me, forcing me to wake up. *Maybe I can manifest the same power?*

"That is a great question, Lin! I'll be back in a few minutes. I need to try something." I head back to Claudette's bedside, hoping that my love can have the same impact on her.

Here goes nothing. In my quest to connect with my emotions, I find myself fixated on one particular feeling: my overwhelming love for Claudette. Her smile, infectious and radiant, lights up the room whenever she enters. *There are so many reasons why I love her.* Letting the feelings engulf me, a luminescent white orb materializes in my hand, emanating a soft buzzing sound. I direct it toward her still form; a lingering vibration tingles through my fingertips as I release the orb, merging it into her body as gently as possible. Her entire body glows with a warm light, her chest rising and falling with each breath, but she doesn't open her eyes. My shoulders slump in defeat. "What am I doing wrong?" As my voice echoes through the air, a burst of magic surges from my body, filling the surroundings with a spectacle of white and gold lights.

Everyone rushes into my room, wearing worried expressions.

Lin places a hand on my shoulder. "Eli, she needs time to heal. She did this to herself."

"In the meantime, we need to devise a plan of attack to defeat Kevin and his tribe of maggots," Adam warns.

"We *need* Claudette to be at full strength when that happens," I argue.

"I agree. However, Claudette cannot help us now," Adam replies.

"How do you propose we defeat Kevin and his followers without her?" I ask.

"I think we should strategize an attack on his territory at night," Lin suggests.

"I second that," Billie says, tapping her fingers together with a callous grin. "Get those little bastards when it's nighttime when they least expect it. I'm talking two or three in the morning."

"I think that's a solid plan," Adam chimes in.

Caron nods in agreement and adds, "Catching them off guard should work."

The group collectively nods.

"It is settled then. We will launch a surprise attack in the dead of night." I glance at each of their unwavering faces. "We all have our own Ce-Ja daggers ready, right?" I ask, receiving nods of confirmation from everyone. "We will use the daggers to eliminate their powers. Who else is fighting with us?"

The group looks around at each other.

"You know how this town is. Besides Isabel, Destiny, and Jessie, I don't see anyone else joining us," Lin says.

My brows snap together, creating a deep furrow on my forehead. "What about Principal Deanwall? This town is brimming with witches and warlocks, and no one wants to rid our home of all this evil?"

"Billie, Jessie, Adam, and I are the only ones willing to get our hands dirty," Caron replies, rubbing her hands together.

"I'm going to head home and grab my spell books," Billie announces.

"We need all the help we can get," Adam adds.

Billie and Adam share a knowing nod as she exits the room.

The fate of this town falls on Claudette's and our shoulders. That is a heavy burden for us; however, we must protect our home.

"We need Chance's Earth ring to locate the book. We may need it for the battle." Adam says.

I collect the ring from Claudette's nightstand and hand it to Adam before he leaves.

"I am going to grab more potions from my shelf. I also need to place another protection spell on the apartment until Claudette wakes up." Caron meets my gaze. "We will defeat them. Don't you worry," she reassures me before following Adam out the door.

Despite her encouraging words, I am worried. *What if Claudette doesn't wake up?* What are we going to do? How will we defeat Kevin without her? Claudette is the most powerful being in this world. She is our only hope against him, and without her, our chances are slim—she just needs to learn to channel her love and not her rage.

Lin sits on the sofa beside me, flipping through Netflix. I try to focus on the TV, but my mind keeps wandering back to Claudette. Pulling myself up from the sofa, I check on her again, and there is still no change in her condition. If only I had the power to wake her up like she did for me.

Pressing my lips against her forehead, I whisper, "Please come back to us, Claudette. I love you." She doesn't move. I can't help but think that, somehow, she is aware of my presence, even in her unconscious state.

Sitting by her side, I'm deep in thought. The location spell Caron cast revealed two locations: Kevin's and Ms. Hudson's. Ms. Hudson had Mr. Richardson's Earth ring; perhaps Kevin has his Earth necklace. As for the Earth spell book, where could it be? Shouldn't the spell have shown us its location since it belonged to her dad? A sudden thought crosses my mind.

I walk back to the living room, where Lin is sitting. "Lin, I have a question."

Pausing the show he is watching, he looks up at me, tapping the remote. "What is it?"

"Why didn't the spell work on locating the Earth spell book? It belongs to

Claudette's father."

"He is dead, so the book is passed down to his next of kin, which would be Claudette. The Earth ring will show us where the book is located, though. Adam is working on a spell as we speak," Lin replies matter-of-factly.

My phone rings, and Adam's name flashes on the screen. *Right on time!* I answer the call, and he informs me that the Earth spell book is at Gabriella's house.

Hanging up, I propose a crazy plan.

"So Lin, what do you think about breaking into Gabriella's house and stealing back the book?"

There has to be something in that book that can help wake Claudette.

Lin looks at me like I've lost my mind. "Bro, Claudette is in a coma. Her magic is drained by rage. She will wake up when her body is ready. No spell can change that."

Feeling defeated, I let out an exasperated sigh and place my forehead into my palm. Perhaps all we can do now is wait and hope for the best.

I head back to my room, feeling helpless. Holding Claudette's hand in mine, I whisper. "Please, Claudette, wake up. I love you."

Chapter 16

Awake

Three days later...

A thick fog clouds my vision, creating a blurry atmosphere that makes it hard to distinguish anything. Blinking repeatedly, I finally regain focus, and my surroundings come into view. I am in Eli's arms, his soft snores filling the room. I shake him gently, and his eyes flutter open, adjusting to the sudden brightness.

He rubs his eyes to shake off the remnants of sleep until the realization dawns on him. "Claudette! You are awake!" He kisses my forehead, my nose, and my lips, relief flooding his handsome features. "Thank God! I thought I had lost you," he says, holding me tight.

How long was I out? Opening my mouth to speak, my throat is dry and scratchy, and my voice comes out as a whisper. "H–How." Eli snaps his fingers, and a glass of water materializes. He hands it to me. As I take a sip, I notice the worry lines on his face, and my heart aches at the thought of causing him distress.

"I'm okay, Eli," I manage to say, my voice still raspy. I reach up to touch his cheek, reassuring him that I'm here and safe with him now.

He exhales a long sigh of relief, his shoulders relaxing as he leans in to kiss my forehead once again. "I was so worried," he murmurs into my hair.

Destiny rushes into the room. "Eli, Kevin—Oh! Claudette, you're awake! Thank goodness!" Destiny shouts, her expression shifting from serious to relieved when she sees me sitting up in bed. "You had us all scared," she adds.

My lips form a weak smile as I nod my head.

"You were saying something about Kevin," Eli reminds Destiny.

Destiny nods and continues. "Oh, right! Kevin and his minions just left. We plan to attack them in two days."

I blink, taking in this new information. "How long have I been out?"

Destiny and Eli exchange a look before Destiny answers, "Almost four days." She continues. "Kevin, his parents, Tanya, and Eli's parents have been attacking us every morning, trying to breach Caron's protection spell. We plan to attack Kevin's home at night to end this once and for all. You have two days to regain your strength." She says.

Nodding my head. "I'll be ready."

"Destiny, I need to speak to Claudette privately," Eli requests and Destiny nods, leaving the room with a knowing look.

What's that about?

Once we are alone, his expression turns serious.

"What is it, Eli?" I touch his arm.

"You need to channel your power from love, Claudette," he begins, his tone grave. "Your love for your mother, your father, your friends, and me. You cannot do what you did before."

I open my mouth to speak, but he places a finger on my lips, silencing me. "Let me finish."

His eyes bore into mine. "I get why you killed Ms. Hudson. However, look what it did to you—it knocked you out. I understand the betrayal you felt, but you have to control it. You have to use your love as a source of strength, not your rage."

Shaking my head. "How do you expect me to channel my love when all I feel is anger? I am *still* angry. My *therapist* killed my father. I trusted her, and she took him away from me. The only family I had left, that witch stole that from me!" My breathing quickens, and rage threatens to consume me.

Eli tilts my chin up; his eyes are full of empathy. "When you woke me up from my coma, you showed me that love is stronger than anything. *Love* is what brought us back together. It is a choice, not just a feeling. It's okay to feel angry, but you have the power to choose how you respond to that anger. You can't go around killing everyone who hurts you."

Exhaling slowly. "I know you're right, Eli. I will try to remember this when I face Kevin."

Eli's face drops to a frown, and he sighs. "Claudette, I am serious! It will take a lot of magic to defeat Kevin, and you won't be able to do it if you let your anger control you. You don't win by losing yourself."

"Okay, okay, I hear you." I surrender with my hands up in defeat. "I will do my best to keep a level head and not let my emotions get the best of me."

He's not entirely convinced. Still, he doesn't say anything more.

It's been days since I last felt like myself, and a haunting feeling lingers inside me after taking Ms. Hudson's life. Kevin is the ultimate enemy. He is the source of all my pain. *I want to kill him for everything he has done.*

Eli helps me to my feet, and we head to the living room to regroup with the others. Jessie, Billie, Lin, Destiny, and Isabel are sitting in a circle on the floor brainstorming strategies. Adam and Caron are in the kitchen mixing potions and pouring their contents into numerous bottles.

"Claudette! You're awake! It's great to have you back," Lin says as I join them, and everyone looks at me with a warm smile.

"It feels good to be back," I reply, a small smile forming on my lips. "You guys plan to catch me up on what I've missed?"

Lin begins explaining. "In two days, we will launch an attack on Kevin's home at night. They have been attacking us every morning, so we will repay the favor."

"And we will not fail like they have," Isabel snorts.

"You have to practice conjuring the fireball you used to wake Eli from his coma," Adam instructs. "We need you to incapacitate Kevin long enough for us to stab him with the Ce-Ja dagger to take his magic away and imprison him."

I was on board with the plan until the last part.

"Stabbing him with the dagger won't kill him!" I roll my eyes. *Why does he get to live while my father had to die?*

Caron's eyes widen at my outburst. "Sweetheart, our goal is to remove Kevin's magic, not kill him. We will be the new Witch Council, and our plan is to handle things differently than before by creating a magical prison. We want to end this without any more bloodshed, if possible."

"Claudette, we talked about this," Eli reminds me. "Killing is our *last* resort."

My blood boils at the thought of sparing Kevin's life. "Kevin pretended to love me. He took my virginity. He had my therapist murder my father—the only family I had left—and you expect me to let him live?"

"What gives you the right to take someone's life?" Caron asks, her voice firm.

"What gives him the right to do it?" I retort, my anger rising.

She doesn't reply, and everyone in the room exchanges uncomfortable glances. *How do they expect me to let that demon live after all he's done to me?* I storm to my room, their distinct chatters fading into the background as I slam the door shut behind me.

Pacing back and forth, I struggle to calm the rage burning inside me. I'm not God, and I don't have the authority to decide who lives and who dies. Still, of all people, Kevin is the last person who deserves mercy—he deserves a ruthless death.

Eli barges into my room, arms folded. "Are you ready to practice?"

Is he serious? I am not in the mood to practice magic and use *love* as my inspiration. *Perhaps I can distract him in a different way.*

"How about we practice something else instead?" I suggest, giving him my best sexy eyes.

"What are you doing with your eyes?" He asks, chuckling, breaking his serious exterior.

"I'm trying to distract you." I tempt him by batting my eyelashes. "I think we both could use a different kind of release right now."

Eli clears his throat. "No, Claudette. As much as I want to, and trust me, I do," he says, tugging at the bulge in his pants, and my eyes follow. "We can't. We need to focus. I need you to conjure the same white fireball you used to wake me up."

Sighing dramatically. "Fine. I guess this isn't the right time."

One thing I know about Eli is that if he doesn't want to do something, there's no changing his mind. He has self-control. *Maybe I should learn a thing or two from him.*

He looks at me expectantly to start practicing, and I comply.

Closing my eyes, I try to replicate the white fireball, using *love* as an inspiration and focusing on the energy within me, but it's not working. I attempted it a few more times. Still, nothing happened. Eli watched me patiently as I continued to struggle. This is a lot harder than I thought it would be.

After three hours of unsuccessful attempts, I slumped onto the bed, feeling overwhelmed and overstimulated.

"Maybe we can try again tomorrow," I suggest in defeat.

"No, keep trying. I'll be right back," Eli says, leaving me alone in the room and returning with Caron and Adam.

"Hit me with your best shot," he challenges them, causing my eyes to widen in disbelief.

"Wait, what? W—what are you doing, Eli?" I stammer.

"Motivation," he replies eagerly.

Before I can protest, Adam and Caron join in, holding hands and chanting a spell, conjuring a captivating sphere of swirling purple and gold energy. They aim the sphere at Eli, firing it with precision and knocking him unconscious.

"What did you do to him?!" I gasp, rushing over to Eli's side.

Caron and Adam shrug, exchanging a knowing look.

"We knocked him out. Now wake him up," Caron demands, and she and Adam exit the room.

Eli is annoying. I love him, but seriously, dude, what was he thinking? I have been practicing for hours to replicate the fireball, and I just can't seem to get it right.

Closing my eyes again, I channel all my energy and push myself to manifest the luminous fireball once more. Peeking through my eyelids, nothing seems to be happening. *What am I doing wrong?*

"Channel your love." The faint sound of a woman's voice whispers to me. *Who was that?*

Concentrating even harder, I focus on love. Memories of Eli flood my mind. His unwavering support, his belief in me, and the way he always makes me feel like I can do anything. Newfound sensations of warmth course through my body as I focus on the feeling of love. His gentle touch when we made love, the way he looked at me with adoration, and the safety I felt in his embrace. With these thoughts in mind, my emotions evoke a renewed sense of purpose. I think about the love I have for my parents—they are the pillars of my strength. And my love for my friends—my chosen family. Suddenly, a celestial sphere materializes, emanating a radiant white light.

I did it! With force, I push forward, striking Eli and jolting him awake in an instant.

He blinks rapidly, regaining his bearings as recognition dawns on him, and a grin spreads on his lips. Rushing to him, I plant kisses all over his face. "I did it, babe, I did it!" I squeal between kisses.

Eli wraps his arms around me, pulling me close. "I knew you could do it. I never doubted you for a second," he hums on my lips.

Straddling him, I scold him. "Don't do that again, and that's an order, Elijah Powers."

He chuckles, his hands gripping my waist and his intense gaze meeting mine. "Understood, Claudette Richardson."

Chapter 17

Attack

Flipping through the pages of my Earth spell book, I search for ways to force Kevin into a slumber. There are so many spells in this book that it is hard to determine which spell I should use.

Eli is beside me, thumbing through his book, when suddenly, Lin barges into the room. "We have to go now!"

We dress in comfortable clothing armed with a Ce-Ja dagger in hand and are ready for war.

Destiny and Isabel join Eli and me in one car, and Lin is with Billie, Caron, Jessie, and Adam.

Planning our next move, we park three blocks away from Kevin's residence. Splitting into teams of two, we each take different blocks toward Kevin's apartment. We arrive in front of his home simultaneously, and a bright red light emanates around its barriers. Like us, they placed a protection spell to keep us from breaking in.

Caron gets into position, holding her hands together. "We need to break the protection spell." With each lightning bolt she conjures, her eyes emit a radiant hue of light purple toward the barrier.

"If they weren't able to break through our barriers, how can we break through theirs?" I ask.

"Good always wins," Adam reassures us as if that explains everything.

Good always wins. I repeat silently to myself.

Billie cracks her knuckles and her neck. "Let's get these little bastards!"

Lin exhales slowly, his hands tracing a circular pattern in the air, materializing a captivating purple sphere of energy.

Isabel and Destiny share a knowing glance and follow suit.

"Let's do this!" Destiny shouts.

In an impressive display of teamwork, the three of them charge forward with incredible speed, simultaneously hurling mystical purple fireballs at the force field. Adam and Jessie materialize burning daggers, aiming with precision to weaken the impenetrable barrier. With each strike, the barrier crackles with an electric surge, sending sparks of vibrant explosions that reverberate through the air. Fragments from the magical shield begin to shatter, forcing them to cover their eyes from the blinding light.

With the barrier weakening, Eli and I clasp hands, our magic merging into a powerful force that effortlessly lifts us above the apartment.

"Babe, channel our love," Eli urges as we soar higher and higher.

Nodding, I think about our love. We concentrate hard on our bond, allowing our emotions to intertwine with our magic. Our brows furrow with determination and sweat beads on our foreheads as we pour all our energy into breaking through the remaining fragments of the force field. The last remnants of the barrier shatter with a resounding crack, sending shards of light scattering in all directions.

"I guess their spell wasn't as good as Caron's." Isabel snickers, kicking down the door with force.

"Oh, please. No one can make a potion like me," Caron gloats, emitting her infamous cackle as she charges into the apartment with Isabel, Destiny, and Billie following closely behind.

Mr. and Mrs. Powers and another stranger who looks oddly familiar are waiting for us inside with bleak expressions. *Is that Ms. Hudson's man?*

"You're so predictable," Elizabeth remarks. "We figured you would strike your attack in the middle of the night."

"We have been expecting you," Joseph states, his gaze cold and unwavering.

With a firm grip, Eli clenches his fists as he listens intently to what his parents are saying.

The stranger steps in front of Elizabeth and Joseph, and a grim line forms on his lips as he addresses me directly. "It is a pleasure to meet you! Witch! I'm Malcolm, and this is for Libby!"

Elizabeth, Joseph, and Malcolm join forces against Eli and me, their magic swirling and crackling in the surrounding air, causing my thoughts to scatter. In a state of confusion and vulnerability, I struggle to regain my footing, pondering the mysteries of my own identity and the purpose of my presence in this place.

What is happening? What am I doing here? Who are they?

There's a strange fog clouding my mind, making it difficult to think clearly. The confusion is overwhelming as I try to piece together the puzzle of my existence. Holding my head in my hands, I try to shake off the disorientation, but the answers remain elusive, leaving me feeling lost and alone in this unfamiliar world.

Someone interferes, clasping my hand in theirs. *Who is this?* His touch sends a jolt of recognition through me, snapping me out of the mind-clouding spell they cast over me.

"Their magic doesn't work on me," Eli says, alerting me back to reality. "I protected my mind from their tricks."

That's my man.

Elizabeth throws a tantrum over Eli's interference and retaliates by launching a gust of gold energy directly at him. I swiftly step in front of Eli, shielding him. Conjuring a purple ball of energy in my hands, I deflect Elizabeth's attack and strike her with a powerful blast. The impact knocks Elizabeth off balance, causing her to sprawl to the ground and rendering her unconscious.

Joseph's reaction to what I did to his wife is far from forgiving. A look of fury crosses his face as he forms an orb of energy, its colors shimmering in a mix of purple and gold. The blast hits Eli and me with such force that we are both thrown backward, landing hard on the ground. Excruciating pain shoots through my body as I struggle to get back on my feet. Joseph and Malcolm share a knowing look, their expressions dark and menacing as they prepare to launch another attack. Jeremiah intrudes from the sidelines, and Joseph turns to his oldest son, communicating a silent plea for him to aid in our ultimate downfall. When Joseph is about to fire another blast of energy, Jeremiah steps in front of us, his arms outstretched in a protective stance. The looks on Joseph's and Malcolm's faces are priceless when they realize Jeremiah is on our side and not theirs.

They recover quickly, their expressions turning from shock to fury. Joseph and Malcolm join forces to launch a coordinated attack towards us, hurling orbs of energy in our direction. We brace ourselves for impact, deflecting the orbs with our powers. The air crackles with energy, with orbs and blasts flying in all directions. Our magic clashes with theirs with enough force to knock them out cold, and its impact slams Eli and me to the ground once again.

Jeremiah helps us to our feet.

The fight is far from over.

"Thank you, Jere." Eli thanks Jeremiah, and they share a brotherly nod before Jeremiah ushers us inside Kevin's apartment.

"Hurry! You don't have much time before they find out what I've done and come after me next." Jeremiah shouts, joining Adam and Jessie in the fight against Kevin's parents.

We enter the apartment with caution. The moment we step inside, we are greeted with a lightning bolt striking the floor in front of us. Losing our balance, we stumble backward, barely avoiding the impact.

The twins and Tanya hold hands, reciting a spell. "We call upon the leader of the Shadow World. Give us the strength and the power we need to end the lives of our enemies."

Caron, Isabel, and Destiny are unconscious on the floor. Eli, Lin, and I are on our knees, holding our heads in agony. The vessels in our brains pulsate with intense pressure as if they are about to rupture. *They are giving us aneurysms.* How original. That's my move.

As the pressure builds, the blood vessels in my head throb with pain, weakening my body and blurring my vision. The pain is unbearable. I feel my existence slipping away as I struggle to maintain consciousness until the faint sound of a male's voice breaks through the haze. *"You can do this."*

Forcing my eyes open, I see my friends in need of help. Caron, Isabel, Billie, and Destiny are incapacitated on the floor. Lin and Eli are both clutching their heads in agony. It's up to me to save us all. *I have to stop this.*

Summoning every ounce of strength left in me, I push through the pain and focus on saving my friends. With each slow and steady breath, my determination grows stronger. Mustering all my willpower, I break through the haze and rise to my feet to take charge of the situation. With a clear mind and a steady hand, I manifest a ball of energy, striking Tanya with a powerful blast that sends her flying into the wall and crashing to the floor, unconscious. When Crissy sees Tanya not moving, she focuses her energy on me. She launches a counterattack, firing magical red and gold spheres toward me. However, I deflect Crissy's feeble attack and send the orbs back towards her with even greater force. The impact knocks Crissy off balance and gives me the opportunity to seize control. I channel my powers with *love*.

Concentrating on protecting myself and my friends, a bubble of energy forms around me, its colors shifting between shades of blue, gold, and brown. It acts as a barrier that repels any further attacks while I ascend above Crissy. From my elevated position, I propel my Ce-Ja dagger with precision, piercing into her chest. She passes out from the impact. Marissa retaliates by using her magic to fling Lin across the room, knocking him unconscious. Descending to the floor, I rush to his side, checking his pulse and making sure he is stable.

His pulse is weak but steady.

Marissa targets Eli next, levitating him above us. Her magic brutally stretches his limbs from their sockets, causing him to groan in agony.

"Enough!" I shout, propelling energy forward into Marissa's chest and breaking the spell she has on Eli. He descends, his limbs snapping back into place.

"What are you waiting for? Do it!" Marissa yells. "Go ahead, kill me! You know you want to."

She's taunting me, trying to provoke a reaction. I *want* to kill her!

"Dark Thunder!" she mocks.

Marissa is trying her best to get me to do it. However, when I meet Eli's gaze, I know he will disapprove. It would make me no better than her. Neglecting my anger, I focus on channeling something far more significant— *mercy*. The Ce-Ja dagger from Eli's pocket teleports to my hand, and with a swift movement, I plunge it into Marissa's stomach, knocking her out cold.

Eli's parents, Malcolm, the twins, and Tanya, have been neutralized. It's time for me to face Kevin. *Alone.*

No one else is getting hurt under my watch.

No more innocent lives are at stake.

This fight is between me and Kevin.

The sun is beginning to rise, and I know this is when Kevin will be the most powerful. But I am ready. I will defeat Kevin Evans for my parents, my friends, my boyfriend, and ultimately for myself. This is the final showdown.

"Get everyone out of here!" I shout to Eli. "I'll handle this alone."

Eli helps Caron, Billie, Destiny, and Isabel to their feet. Jeremiah and Adam carry Lin out of the apartment.

With my friends safely out of harm's way, it's finally time for me to confront this menacing demon.

Before exiting the apartment, Eli locks eyes with me, and time stands still for a moment. He mouths, *I love you*, tugging at my heartstrings before evacuating the apartment.

I can do this.

Pacing the apartment, I search for any sign of Kevin. He is hiding in plain sight, waiting for the perfect moment to strike. Still, I am prepared, mentally and physically. "Kevin, come out, come out wherever you are," I tease. "I know you can hear me. It's time you stop lurking in the shadows and face me."

Suddenly, I hear a faint sound that comes from behind me, causing me to spin around quickly, only to find that there is nothing there. A sinister sneer hangs in the air, unsettling my senses. Again, I call out into the empty room, feeling his lingering presence taunt me. There's more movement, this time louder, and I see a flicker of a shadow out of the corner of my eye. With caution, I pivot on my heels, my heart beating rapidly in my chest, only to find myself engulfed in an eerie darkness yet again. Kevin is playing mind games with me. I turn back around and nearly jump out of my skin when I see him walking through the wall behind me. In his complete demon form, his beady black eyes glint with malice as he approaches, a chilling smirk on his face. My breath catches in my throat, and I stumble backward. The sight of his intimidating presence causes goosebumps to rise on my skin. Black claws extend from his fingertips, two prominent horns protrude from his head, and a distorted face leers at me. There is no trace left of the handsome man I was once deeply in *love* with. The demon before me is frightening and unrecognizable, a stark contrast to the person I thought I knew. With a wave of his hand, a force pushes me through the wall and into a room I don't recognize. A shooting pain sears through my body as I hit the floor, adding to the confusion that grips me. Kevin grasps me by the throat and flings me across the room, again and again, until I am barely conscious, giving me no chance to heal myself.

Why did I think I could beat a demon?

He launches at me again, but this time, I manage to summon a burst of energy and hurl it back at him. It has no impact on him whatsoever.

Um, what? With each breath, I gather my strength and unleash a series of energy blasts in his direction, which does nothing to him.

"You'll never win!" With every word he utters, his voice rumbles like a deep growl. The sound of his voice is bone-chilling, almost as if it's not his voice at all. *He sounds like a monster.*

"I won," he snarls, grabbing hold of my hair. "And now I will kill you."

The force of his punch connects with my nose, causing bones to crunch and blood to splatter, creating a horrifying scene. I hit the floor hard, struggling to stay conscious. Kevin conjures a flaming red and orange fireball, penetrating the searing force into my chest, causing me to gasp for air as darkness impairs my vision. The pain is like a thousand knives stabbing into my body all at once. Holding on by a thread, I can feel my strength waning. The room is spinning around me, making it difficult for me to see clearly. Leaning my head back against the cold floor, a sinking feeling tells me that this might be my final moment.

I don't have the strength to defeat him.

I am not the most powerful being to walk this Earth.

This is how I will meet my end.

My eyelids grow heavy, and I think I am starting to see the light at the end of the tunnel. This is it! The light is beautiful, peaceful, and inviting. I slowly reach out my hand, and the radiant white light seems to be beckoning me towards it, flooding every corner of my sight. My body floats toward the bright light, and the soft hum of energy resonates in the fresh air around me; I can almost taste the purity of the ethereal glow. I continue to reach towards it, a comforting warmth enveloping me like a gentle embrace from the great divine. *Is this the Light World?*

Two silhouettes, a woman and a man, appear in the distance. They seem familiar, but their faces are masked. They gently touch my shoulders, chanting in unison, "We call upon the Earth's greatest power to defeat the demon in this hour. Give her the strength that she needs to annihilate our enemy."

A force instantly snaps me out of my thoughts and brings me back to the present moment; my soul returns to my body, fully aware of my surroundings.

Kevin is now hovering over me, wielding a dagger above my heart. Time freezes still for a brief moment just as he is about to dive the dagger into my skin. I swiftly grab his wrist with both my hands, pushing the blade away with all my might. His demonic eyes stare into mine with pure hatred, and mine mirror back with defiance. He pushes back with equal force, both of us trying to gain the upper hand. I squirm and twist, using every ounce of strength to keep the dagger at bay. It is just inches away from my neck now; the sunlight rising is glinting off its sharp edge. The blade grazes my flesh, drawing a thin line of blood. *My hands are confined, but my legs are free.* Bending my knees, I kick my legs upward with force. He lets go of my wrist, and I am able to wrap my legs around his neck and use all my power to pull him down to the floor and spin, pinning him beneath me. The dagger clatters to the floor near our entangled bodies. He stretches his hand out, reaching for the blade. I channel the Earth's energy to maintain my advantage and keep him subdued under me, grabbing the dagger before he can reach it. His own weapon is now pressed against his throat, nipping at his skin. *The tables have turned.*

It takes everything in me to resist the urge to end him right here and now, as opposed to neutralizing his magic. He deserves it after all the pain he has caused me, and the bitter look in his beady eyes tells me he knows it, too.

"I will kill you," he spits out, a distorted smirk twisting his lips.

Taking his life would only make me just like him, and I refuse to let him have that satisfaction. Instead, I think about my love for my parents, my friends, and my boyfriend, who are all counting on me to make the right choice and end this without losing myself in the process.

"Not today," I reply, a small smile forming on my lips. Exhaling a sharp breath, I muster all of my strength and resolve, choosing to channel love and not rage. Throwing his weapon to the other side of the room, I then open and close my free hand, summoning the Ce-Ja dagger to my side, and with one swift strike, I stab the blade into his neck, watching as his eyes widen in shock. Red smoke expels from his body, and he twists and turns, reverting back to the familiar form of the man I once knew.

EARTH

Standing to my feet, panting heavily, I exhale and wipe the sweat from my forehead.

It's over, I won!

Chapter 18

Peace

Eight weeks later...

Dear Diary,

Life is great! Eli and I are doing fantastic. I love him more every day, and he loves me just as much. Eli makes me so happy, and he is not using me for an evil plan. Yeah, I know I'm still working on letting it go! The summer is almost over, and I look forward to my senior year of high school in a few weeks.

I have learned so much at Mashal High and can't wait to continue studying in college next year. My plan is to attend SME University once I graduate from Mashal High. There are three schools: one for warlocks, one for witches, and one for both. Eli and I have decided to attend the same school; we are not enrolling in the same classes, though. That would be too much. I love him, but I don't need to see him at home and in all my classes. Now, let's get to the good part—my enemies.

Kevin and all his trusted minions are now locked away in an impenetrable magical prison, thanks to Caron—Mashalville's Potions Master. And Adam conjured cuffs that dampened magic. Even though all of their magic was removed with the Ce-Ja dagger, it's better to be safe than sorry.

The new Witch Council consists of Eli, Lin, Adam, Jessie, Caron, and me. Destiny stepped down as a Witch Council member to spend more time with Isabel. We have meetings on Fridays to discuss all things magical. There is a greater evil brewing out in the atmosphere, and we are keeping our eyes peeled should we need to get involved. Our goal is to protect Mashalville from all threats.

We found out that Elizabeth Powers was behind the deaths of Destiny's mother and Isabel's parents. Destiny's mother, as well as Isabel's parents, got caught investigating Earth witch killings, and Elizabeth admitted her involvement in silencing them. The police in this town are no longer under Elizabeth's influence, and I hope she and her husband rot in prison for the rest of their lives. Jeremiah and Eli are closer than ever now that their parents got the punishment they deserved. Jeremiah even joined the police force as a rookie.

Oh, and Lin's parents... Kevin's mother confessed to killing them on behalf of Antus. Eli's suspicions were correct. That poor woman is so disoriented— she has not been in control of her own thoughts or actions. I had a notion that something was off about her the very first time I met her. The Witch Council deliberated and decided on a lighter sentence for her due to her mental state and the influence of Antus. She received a five-year prison sentence, and her husband agreed to serve his time until his very last breath. His words, not mine.

With the twins in prison, Gabriella and I have been on civil terms. She apologized for being an awful stepmother and wished she had done things differently. There was remorse in her eyes. Sometimes, I wonder what life would have been like if things had turned out differently between us. It's not like she forced me to do chores or be the housemaid... she was just unkind to me, and, of course, she did try to kill me with peanuts that one time. I know, I know. Water under the bridge.

It's been so long since I've actually been happy. I still miss my parents every day, but the pain no longer weighs me down like it used to. I accept they are gone, and I know I will see them again one day. Ms. Cameau, my guidance counselor from my previous high school, schedules phone call sessions with me once a week to check-in, and the Witch Council is okay with my two best friends knowing about magic. I am still working on convincing them to let Mitch know as well. This may take some time.

As far as school goes, the mags and the norms now interact more freely. I didn't enjoy being a part of a school implementing modern-day segregation among its students. It wasn't a great idea years ago, and it's not a great idea now!

Eli barges into my room with a goofy grin on his face. "Babe, I have done it!"

Closing my diary and hiding it underneath my pillow, I tilt my head to the side. "What have you done?"

"Follow me," he says, grabbing my hand and pulling me out of the room.

I follow him to the living room, curious about what he could be so excited about.

Our friends are sitting on the floor and gathered in a circle, each holding a flickering candle. Adam and Caron sit in the center, holding hands. They have broad grins on all of their faces.

My brows snap together. "What is this, Eli? What's going on?"

He turns to me with a grin, kissing me on the cheek. "This is your victory against the greater evil's surprise!"

Bursting into laughter. "My what?"

"You defeated Kevin! That's huge!" Eli lifts me up and spins me around in circles, and my friends cheer us on. "This is your present from all of us," he says, placing me back down on the floor. "You deserve it."

Joining my friends on the floor, I sit cross-legged and smile from ear to ear. Anticipation fills my heart as I wait to see what surprise they have planned for me.

Eli pulls out a crumpled piece of paper from his pocket. He unfolds it and reads aloud, "In this sacred hour, we call upon the leader of the Light World to allow us time with the ones Claudette loves and honors."

Everyone else joins in, chanting in unison two more times, their words echoing through the dimly lit room.

Adam and Caron pass out when the spell is complete, and the lights flicker, casting a mystical glow around us. A haunting and pungent scent fills the room, and white smoke billows out from the center of the circle, forming two figures that look eerily familiar. The air becomes frigid, and a brisk wind cuts through me, biting at my skin and sending shivers down my spine. The smoke begins to dissipate, and the two distinct figures—a man and a woman—emerge from the haze. I blink repeatedly, rubbing my eyes to make sure I'm not hallucinating. *I'm not!* A wave of shock washes over me, hitting me like a ton of bricks—*it's my mom and dad!*

I slowly rise to my feet; however, they feel like they're glued to the floor. Overwhelmed with emotions, I stand there paralyzed, struggling to process the surreal sight of my parents magically morphing into living flesh-and-blood beings right before my eyes. The tears well up in my eyes, and the realization hits me like a thunderbolt—they're back from the dead!

Tears stream down my cheeks. "What is happening?! This can't be real."

Eli steadies me with a reassuring hand on my shoulder, his voice calm as he says, "I know it's hard to believe, but they're really here. Caron and Adam are temporarily taking your mother and father's place in the Light World. The crossover process is almost complete."

His words sink in, and my mouth goes dry. This is really happening!

"We will give you some privacy," he says when the crossover is complete.

My mother and father step forward, their faces filled with love and familiarity.

"Mom! Dad!" I rush forward, tears streaming down my face as I embrace them.

"How is this possible? How are you here?" I ask through choked sobs. "I am so sorry for everything. I–"

My father kisses my forehead, cutting me off. "It's okay, Cheetah. We saw everything. We understand."

"Daddy," I wail, sobbing into his chest, and he squeezes me tighter.

My mother cups my face in her hands, wiping away my tears. "We are so proud of you, my darling daughter. We have been watching over you all this time. You have grown into such a strong and beautiful person." She says, smiling.

I missed her smile; she is so beautiful.

I grasp her hands, bringing them to my nose and inhaling her familiar scent. I have missed her so much. "Mommy," I choke out, my voice cracking with emotion.

"I miss you, too, sweetheart," she says, kissing our clasped hands. "I know how much pain you have felt without me by your side, but know that I am always with you, guiding you every step of the way."

A thought occurs to me, and I swallow hard. "Was that you on the day of the train incident?"

She nods, her eyes glistening with tears. "Yes, my love. The veil was open that day and I was able to change the train tracks to keep you safe. I will always protect you, no matter what."

"And it was you two who helped me defeat Kevin?" I ask, already knowing the answer.

They nod in response, and more tears fall from my eyes. I can't stop crying.

My parents hug me tight, soothing me with their love.

"Cheetah, don't cry. You are never alone," my father says while my mother strokes my hair.

"We don't have much time left." Her voice fills with sadness. "I love you so much, my darling daughter." She kisses my forehead, and my father squeezes us into a bear hug.

"We will always be with you, although we're not physically here," he says.

I wipe my tears and smile at them. "I love you both so much. I will miss you every single day." The weight of their impending departure settles in my chest, and I try to hold back the flood of emotions threatening to overwhelm me.

"We will miss you too, sweetheart," my mother says, her eyes brimming with unshed tears.

"But we will always be watching over you," my father adds.

Despite the lump in my throat, I try to maintain my composure.

"One more thing, sweetheart," my mother says, smiling through her tears. "We love Eli. He is definitely a keeper."

My heart swells. Their blessing means everything to me.

With one last hug, they release me, and I step back as they disappear into the haze of smoke.

I drop to my knees, tears streaming down my face—tears of happiness, not sorrow.

Caron and Adam wake up from their slumber, and Eli and my friends return to the living room.

"Thank you! Thank you so much for this wonderful gift! I don't know how to express how much this means to me." I squeal, overwhelmed with gratitude. "I love you all so much."

"We love you too, and we are so glad to see you happy," Destiny says with a smile, wrapping her arms around me, and everyone joins in for a group hug.

I love these people! They are my chosen family, and I am beyond blessed to have them in my life.

Two days later...

Eli and I are at the prison gates.

"Are you sure you want to do this today?" Eli brushes his lips against mine.

"Yes, I need to do this," I reply, gripping his hand. "I'm ready."

He squeezes my hand in silent support. "Okay, Claudette. I'll be right here waiting for you when you come out."

"Thank you, babe." I plant my lips on his one last time before heading down the long corridor towards the staircase.

Descending ten levels below the prison, a wave of anxiety washes over me as I approach the heavy metal door leading to Kevin's cell.

When his gaze meets mine, his brows rise in surprise. There are noticeable dark circles under his eyes, and his face looks older than before.

"What brings you here, Claudette?" He asks, spitting into a mason jar he keeps by his cot.

I take a deep breath, trying to steady my nerves. Inching closer to the cell bars, I muster the courage to speak. "Why did you do it?"

"Do *what*?" He smirks, a bitter edge to his voice. "I need you to be more specific."

Confronting him head-on, I look him straight in the eye and ask, "Why did you go through the trouble of dating me?"

Kevin chuckles, the sound echoing off the cold stone walls. Rising from his cot, he pushes his face against the metal bars, his gaze cold and calculating. "That's why you came to visit me?"

I can see the hatred and resentment in his eyes. Taking a step back, I steady myself and reply, "Yes, that's why I'm here."

"Very well, Claudette. It won't be pretty," he warns, rubbing his dirty fingernails against his shirt. "I never loved you. I never cared about you. I only wanted my magic back. You were just a pawn in my game." He pauses for my reaction, but I have none. "You were nothing to me," he continues. "And every time we had sex, I was thinking about Tanya." He pauses again, waiting for my response. I won't give him the satisfaction. "I was thrilled when your father was murdered. It meant I was one step closer to getting what I wanted.

You were just a means to an end." He laughs coldly, finishing his cruel confession.

I simply stare at him, blinking. His words have no effect on me now. I needed to hear him say it with his own mouth.

With a calm voice, I say, "Thank you for finally being honest with me," and I turn on my heel to walk away, leaving him alone in his own bitterness.

"That's it?!" He calls out after me, gripping the metal bars. "You're just going to walk away?"

I don't look back.

"These bars won't hold me forever! I will get my magic back again. You have not won, Claudette!"

My feet come to a sudden halt, and for a split second, I consider turning back. However, I don't.

"Good always wins!" I shout over my shoulder, and with a wave of my hand, I close the door behind me with a resounding clang.

The End

Thank you for reading Claudette's story!
But wait!! There's more.

All good things must come to an end. However, the end marks the start of an exciting new journey.
Keep reading for a sneak peek into the enchanted realm of Jajuville!

If you enjoyed Earth, please consider leaving a review on Amazon, Goodreads,

BookBub, or anywhere else. By spreading the word, you can help support an indie author. Reviews are extremely important.

Welcome to the enchanting realm of Jajuville.

Separated at birth, fraternal twins Josephine and Marie will reunite on their eighteenth birthday. One twin has the power of fire; the other has the power of ice. However, what should have been a joyous reunion takes an unexpected turn when they least expect it. An evil threat known as the Shadow King plans to sacrifice the twins on their birthday. The twins must join forces, harness their unique abilities, and cooperate for the greater good.

Can they rise above their contrasting perspectives and find common ground?

Join the Toussaint Sisters on an adrenaline-pumping adventure as they face off against the most formidable villain in the enchanted realm of Jajuville.

Kindly be aware that this Young Adult Dark Fantasy does not adhere to the traditional Happily Ever After narrative and is associated with the Magic is Real series.

Introduction to

One thousand years ago, two brothers fell ill, their bodies succumbing to the ravages of disease. Their mother, desperate to save them, performed an ancient ritual that miraculously healed her sons and bestowed upon them extraordinary abilities. They soon became powerful brothers, each with their own distinct personalities and strengths. As they continued to age, one of them started embracing evil, while the other chose the path of goodness.

Antus had grand ambitions, aspiring to be worshipped as a god and dominate the entire world. On the other hand, Jaju had a simple desire—he wanted his people to have a life filled with serenity. The two were at odds, unable to find common ground on their purpose.

Jaju desired to create a realm where witches could reside, while Antus aspired to rule over the real world along with the witches.

After years of resentment, fights, and exposure to the humans, Jaju went on to create Jajuville, the Magical Realm, where his people were gifted with the powers of Fire and Ice. At the same time, Antus and his followers were trapped in Mashalville.

Antus became a formidable threat, prompting witches to unite in a mission to eliminate him and condemn him to the Shadow World. He placed his curse on the Sun, Moon, and Earth witches for banishing him there. Every child born from the same coven was engulfed with darkness and forced to serve Antus, granting him the ability to seek revenge on Jaju and his people by creating the very first Shadow King from beyond the grave. In doing so, the magical veil was broken, and the people of Mashalville were able to leave if they wanted to. The people of Mashalville needed order, and the Powers family was the first family to form the Witch Council and set their rules in place.

Pierre was tired of living in the shadow of his twin brother and made a dark deal with the Shadow King that Antus created. Pierre didn't know that he would be the very first twin to merge, causing him to remain young and alive for decades.

It is time for another merger. Will he succeed in killing and absorbing Josephine and Marie's powers on their eighteenth birthday?

Brace yourself for the upcoming release of Fire and Ice: The Toussaint Sisters. . . (TBA)

Thank you for purchasing Earth! I hope you have enjoyed my story as much as I enjoyed writing it.

Let's be friends!

Please find me on any of the social media platforms below and join my newsletter.

My website: https://kcmcmillian.mailchimpsites.com/

Newsletter: https://eepurl.com/iJtSzA

Instagram: www.instagram.com/kcminspired_author

My Broadcasting Channel on Instagram:

https://ig.me/j/AbbtqGM3rQEE4wwD/

Facebook: www.facebook.com/kcmcmillianauthor

Facebook Group:

https://www.facebook.com/groups/931639820833941/

TikTok: www.tiktok.com/@kcminspired_author

GR: www.goodreads.com/author/show/22481124.K_C_McMillian

Books by K.C. McMillian

- Bright A Forbidden Love Story, available now.
- Seventeen Magic is Real Part I, available now.
- Earth Magic is Real Part II, available now.
- Magic is Real Special Edition Hardcover, October 7th, 2024.
- Loving Reign: A Fake Dating Romance Novel (Book One) 18+ and older coming February 2025!
- The Forbidden Fruit Tales of the Remi Clan (The Nosis Series) 18+ and older (TBA)
- Fire & Ice: The Toussaint Sisters (TBA)

ACKNOWLEDGMENTS

Thank you for taking a chance on me. I really hope you enjoyed reading Claudette's story and the sneak peek at Fire and Ice.

Huge thanks to Shalinie Rohit for once again joining me on this journey.

Thank you to my wonderful husband, Troy, for all of your support and for being my true love. I love you with my all.

Thank you, Amy Sobel, for all of our chats, your encouraging words, and your support. Thank you for always being on my side.

Thank you so much, Alicia Marcia, for joining me on this journey and for your support and encouragement.

I love all of you!

Special Thanks

To my awesome ARC readers whom I asked to share

Earth Magic is Real cover reveal to their Instagram pages.

Thank you, guys so much for highlighting my book!

Zowie Norris @zowie_norris_author

Brooke Young   @murraysmiraculousmission

Rudrashree Makwana @reviewsbyrudra

Anjuri Mehrotra @booknerdy2020

Sarah Thompson O Sullivan @_thelostlibrary_

Rhyz Larrucea @rhyzkhua.reads

ABOUT THE AUTHOR

When Kiana "K.C." McMillian was a child, she would make up stories in her head and write them down. While attending high school, her favorite play was Romeo and Juliette, and she enjoyed reading it, but she sometimes fumbled over her words while reading in front of her classmates. And, of course, children can be cruel. Kiana didn't like being made fun of and lacked confidence in herself, and she felt that if she couldn't read in front of a crowd, then perhaps she wasn't good enough to write. She didn't think her stories would be well received and feared failing at something she loved. Kiana knew back then that she would one day want to share her imagination with others, but she wasn't sure about putting herself out there.

Fast forward twenty years later, after the death of her husband's grandmother on January 13th, 2022, she decided she wouldn't let the fear of failure hinder her from following her dreams. Before "Gran," as she and her husband called her, left this Earth, she said, "I have lived my life, and I've done everything I wanted to do; I'm ready." K.C. knew that if her life suddenly came to a tragic end, she wouldn't be satisfied. That statement inspired her, and she decided to follow her dream of becoming an author.